Last
One Home

Last
One Home

Mary Pope Osborne

 D I A L   B O O K S
New York

PUBLISHED BY DIAL BOOKS

2 Park Avenue / New York, New York 10016
Published simultaneously in Canada
by Fitzhenry & Whiteside Limited, Toronto
Copyright © 1986 by Mary Pope Osborne

Library of Congress Cataloging-in-Publication Data

Osborne, Mary Pope. Last one home.
Summary: Twelve-year-old Bailey struggles with her
feelings of loneliness after her parents' divorce when
her father plans to remarry and her brother prepares
to leave for the service.
[1. Remarriage—Fiction. 2. Brothers and
sisters—Fiction.] I. Title.
PZ7.O81167Las   1986   [Fic]   85-20588
ISBN 0-8037-0219-1

Printed in the U.S.A.
Design by Sara Reynolds
First Edition
W
2 4 6 8 10 9 7 5 3 1

for Natalie, John, and Will Boyce

With special thanks to my mother, Barnette Pope, for providing me with a workplace to write much of this book; to my agent, Shelly Fogelman, and my editor, Amy Ehrlich, for their continuing encouragement and direction; and to my husband, Will, as always, for his wonderful help and support

Last
One Home

One

Two things are happening soon: Daddy's getting married and Claude's going in the Army. A week from tomorrow Daddy's marrying his girlfriend, Janet, and the very next day, June 28, Claude has to report for boot camp in Tallahassee.

I might just be Claude's twelve-year-old sister, but sometimes I feel more like his mother. "Hey, you poor thing," I say to him as the two of us sit on the couch in front of *60 Minutes*. Daddy and Janet and her stinko twin boys just left for Janet's house. "If you're dreading the Army, just think how it'll be for me—living with Janet and Petey and Buster. Here—want some gum?"

"I'm not dreading the Army," Claude mumbles as he takes a stick of Dentyne from me.

"Sure." I watch him put the gum in his mouth. His

long thin legs sprawl out so far in front of him that
his sock feet nearly touch the TV. I lean over and pat his
head and go, "Whoo—whoo—"

Sometimes I act like an ape from the movie *Tarzan*
just for the excuse to touch Claude's head. I like his
sweet, sweaty hair; it was like new grass when he was
younger. He's got to be sitting down or lying on the sofa,
though, for me to touch his hair, because he's six feet
five inches tall. Claude just shot into the sky one month
last summer—grew so tall in such a short period of time
that it hurt his breathing. Plus he's skin and bones.
Daddy likes to tease him, saying his chest looks like it's
already been hit by a mortar shell, all sunk in the way it
is. But to me it looks sweet: a young man's hairless skin.
The United States Army won't see it that way, though,
you can be sure of that. Suddenly I smack his head.

"Oww, Bailey! Cut it out!" he says.

"Oh, Petey, honey—are you hurt? Are you all right?"
I say, imitating the way Janet sounded this afternoon
when I pushed one of her six-year-old twins into the
bushes and he got a scratch on his arm—a teeny one,
you can be sure.

Claude can't help but laugh. The two of us spend
about half our time making each other laugh. "How
come you always give Janet a hard time?" he says.

"I'm trying to expose her."

"What are you trying to expose?"

"That she's a witch—"

"She is not."

"You wanna bet? Under that sweet exterior she's a
wild witch."

"You're crazy."

"Wait and see. She'll lose it sooner or later. Then I better *watch out!*" I move in on Claude, raking the air with my fingers like I'm a monster.

"Cut it out," he says, laughing.

"She'll destroy me!" I yell, and I start to pummel his head.

"Quit! Stop!" he says, grabbing my hands. He wrestles me off the couch, then keeps me away from him with his feet and legs. I pull off one of his socks and start whipping him with it.

"Okay, stop now," he says, holding up his hand. "That's enough. Quit. Quit."

I sock whip him around the head a little more.

"C'mon. Give me my sock."

"Go and get it." I toss it across the room.

"Okay. Leave me alone now," he says. "I want to watch the TV."

"Hey, I've got a good idea. Let's go to the pier and sit for a while."

Claude holds up his hand, telling me to be quiet. Mike Wallace is going on about some crooked doctor in California—who cares?

I plop down on the couch and sigh loudly and play with my gum wrapper. Daddy will spend the night at Janet's again tonight, I'm sure. Next Tuesday after the two of them get married, he's moving over to her house for good; and I'm supposed to go with him. That's why the coffee table's gone from this room, and our stereo, and our oil painting of Elvis Presley. Daddy's already taken them to Janet's, along with all our records and his gun collection. He takes something every time he leaves. Why, today all four of them marched out of here carrying our entire set of *World Books*. You think I helped? Ha.

In fact, Daddy's a little irritated because me and Claude haven't been helping with the packing. He keeps telling us to go to the supermarket and get some boxes and start loading our things into them, but we seem to keep forgetting.

"Hey." I kick Claude's old bony knee. "Don't you want to go to the pier? Come on, this is boring. Let's take a ride to the beach. Let's go before it gets dark." I jump down like an ape, gesturing for him to come. "Whoo? Whoo?"

"Bailey, they're going to lock you up if you don't watch it," he says.

"Who cares? An institution's a better place to live than Janet's."

"Yeah? You think so? Try it sometime."

"I have."

"Oh yeah?"

"Sure. I know what it's like from visiting Mom. It was nice."

"Oh. Well, you go there, but don't expect me to visit you."

I just look at him. That was Claude's attitude about Mom too, except she wasn't in an institution for crazies; it was a place for alcoholics. That was just before she left us for good three and a half years ago.

Claude heaves himself up off the couch and picks up his sock. He balances himself awkwardly and pulls it on; then he steps into his loafers. "Come on, before you drive *me* crazy," he says.

"Yippee," I say. I run to my room and grab one of my fishing caps; then I follow Claude out of the house as he walks slump shouldered ahead of me like some old sorrowful giant.

Actually, I know Claude feels sad about leaving me next week, but Claude's the type who makes you circle gently around his deepest feelings—it's dangerous to go for them directly. Once I read about this environmentalist who picked up an endangered baby condor to try to save it, and the bird died right there in the man's hand of a heart attack. I've often imagined how terrible it must have felt to hold that rare baby bird and feel its heart thumping like crazy against your fingers, and then feel it stop. That's why I handle Claude so gently—I know how sensitive he is underneath.

Outside I catch up to him and slap him hard on the back. I don't even come up to Claude's shoulders. I haven't nearly come into my full growth yet; in fact, I'm quite small for my age. But I figure it'll hit me some summer like it did him: *whoosh*, and I'll go from being four feet eight inches to being seven feet tall. Watch out.

"Are you a little nervous about boot camp?" I ask, snapping my gum.

He shrugs.

"I would be. Lotta mean fellows, I bet."

He makes a face.

"Really! You know, those kind of sergeants that make you clean the bathrooms with a toothbrush—"

"Don't worry about it," he says.

"I'm not worried!" I pop a little gum bubble as I watch him unlock his car door. "You're the one who should worry—you're the one marching willingly toward hell. How come you're asking for misery?"

He smiles at me. "You're not going to make me change my mind," he says.

"You're not going to make me change my mind," I mimic him as I get into the car and slam my door.

Claude signed up for the Army right after he and his old girlfriend, Marlene McKinney, broke up. That was about a month ago. I can't imagine what Marlene could have done that made him desperate enough to do that. I know she still cares for him too, because she keeps calling our house. But Claude's always making me give her some excuse, and I hate doing it—Marlene was practically a member of our family for a whole year! But I don't dare ask him about her anymore. If I just hint that I'd like to know more about what happened between the two of them, he about bites my head off.

"Hey. Listen to this." I look over at him as he starts up the car. "If you stayed here, maybe we could move somewhere together—just the two of us. We could move to the Everglades!"

He gives me an amused look like I'm just a squeaky mouse or something. I give him a severe look back and say, "I'm serious now, Claude!"

He wrinkles his brow, pretending to look real serious.

"Oh, eat dog doo," I tell him, and I turn my head to look out the window.

.   .   .

When we get to the pier, we buy a couple of Cokes from the drink machine and walk out to sit on a bench in the twilight. An old couple's fishing near us. They're both wearing crinkled cotton hats and the man's smoking a cigar while the woman pours something out of a thermos into two paper cups. Her rod's stuck in a hole on the wooden rail, fishing by itself.

"We should try fishing again," I say to Claude.

"Yeah."

"I wish you weren't leaving, so we could fish some this summer. I wish we could go camping someplace and live off the land, don't you?"

He doesn't answer. I might have danced a little too close to his feelings this time, but I want him to think about that summer when the two of us spent all our time fishing together in this bad-smelling putty-colored stream near our house. One day in late August a police-man stopped and told us it was polluted, but that was okay—we never caught diddly squat there anyway except for a few catfish we threw back in. That was the summer before our mother left. It was her worst time; she drank all day every day and watched the television. Sometimes she'd put on tons of makeup and call taxis to come and get her—but when they came, she wouldn't know what they were there for. None of us knew what to do. Daddy had about given up by then. Every day Claude would lead me down to that ugly stream to get away from the house and Mom. It would be hot and the mosquitoes would eat us alive, but he'd make it into an adventure. We pretended we were living by ourselves, off the land.

"Look at that silly bunch of nuts today," I say, pointing toward the pelicans that like to sit on the roof of the little shelter at the end of the pier. There's about ten of them sitting there, some all squashed down and puffed out. There's a couple of them with yellow fuzz on their heads. I've seen that before, but I don't know what it means. "How come those two have yellow fuzz on their heads?" I ask Claude.

"They're trying to look punk," he says.

That about kills me. I whoop and shake with laughter. "That's good," I say.

You might not believe this, but Claude and I actually *petted* the head of a pelican last winter! Really. I wasn't afraid to do that—you can just sense that pelicans are a lot tougher than condors. I loved it. I'll always remember the feel of that pelican's tiny wet head—the sweet bird just stood there on the pier, ducking a little as we patted him gently. I'd like to go off and study birds someday, maybe specialize in pelicans, be a kind of bird doctor who mends their beaks or wings or feet. "What would be your ideal occupation?" I ask Claude. "If you could be anywhere, be anybody, what would it be?"

He thinks for a moment, then says, "Remember that job Uncle John had in Virginia Beach?"

"When he worked in the lighthouse and talked to the ships about the weather and all?"

"Yeah."

"That would be your ideal job?"

He nods.

That makes sense. Claude likes to listen to his short-wave radio for news of storms and weather disasters, and he clips out newspaper stories about big hurricanes and tornadoes, and he's the only person I've ever heard of who can spend hours in front of the all-weather channel on cable TV. That's fun entertainment as far as he's concerned!

"How come the weather interests you so much?" I ask him.

"I don't know. It just does."

"I guess it is pretty interesting. My fifth-grade teacher told us about this girl who saw a tornado coming and she jumped in a ditch, and it passed right over her and didn't bother her a bit except it took *all the hair off her body.*"

"Bailey, you've told me that story about ten times."

"But it's interesting every time, isn't it?"

He laughs and says no.

"You know what would be my ideal thing to do?" I say.

"What?"

"Frankly I'd like it if Daddy didn't get married and if you didn't go in the Army, and if just the three of us went off to an island and ran a pelican farm."

"What's that?"

"It's a place I invented where we could take care of hurt pelicans."

"Oh." He keeps looking at me like he doesn't know what to say. Then he grabs me and pulls my fishing cap off and rubs his knuckles back and forth across my skull. We call this a "noogie burn."

"Don't! No!" I say, laughing. When he lets me up, I give him a push.

"Okay, okay," he says.

I settle back on the bench again and point to a fish head covered with flies lying not far from us and say, "Yuk." That's the only thing I don't like about being on this pier—you see fish parts here and there, heads and glistening guts.

"You want to go to McDonald's?" he asks after another minute or two.

"Yeah, sure!" I exclaim, and we get up and walk like two cartoon guys down the pier—a big giant and a little shrimp.

A cool breeze blows through the car as we ride along the ocean. Claude slows down and looks out his window when we pass the teenage area of the beach. I suspect he's looking to see if Marlene's there. I crane my neck to look too, and yep, there she is—playing volleyball with a bunch of boys. Marlene's tall and skinny like Claude, and she has curly auburn hair and freckles. Right now she looks as if she's having a good old time, jumping around and laughing in the fading daylight.

It's hard to tell what Claude's thinking as he drives on, but once we're on the highway, he starts speeding. I think it's because he saw Marlene having fun with a bunch of boys. I'd like to tell him he shouldn't be so upset about that. Marlene's always friendly with everyone—in fact, she was voted the Friendliest Girl in their senior class this year.

The wind blows wildly through the car, and Claude leans forward like he's a maniac who's about to drive us off a cliff into space. "This is fun!" I shout, thinking these might be my last words.

But we make it to McDonald's okay—without a wreck or a ticket, or anything.

Two

I slept all night on the couch on the front porch. I conked out pretty soon after we got back from McDonald's. The last thing I remember was watching the bugs flap around the naked bulb over the front door; and now I'm having to squint my eyes against the hot morning sunlight. My head feels so heavy, I don't mind just lying here on the plastic cover for a minute, looking out at the yard—at the giant yellow allamanda flowers twining through our neighbor's chain link fence. Allamandas are the most yellow thing I know—more yellow than hot dog mustard, spilled raw egg on your clothes—or even the heads of those punk pelicans yesterday. I laugh a little thinking about that comment of Claude's.

My eyes move to a white-winged dove that's walking in the grass near the chain fence—hey, two of them.

You know, a dove's song is supposed to sound like he's saying, "Who-cooks-for-you?" I like that. And I like this time of day when flowers and birds seem in charge. You can hear a few cars and a dog barking, but I don't mind that. My worst time of day is around three o'clock when nothing seems new anymore—when it's boring and hot, and the sky's glaring and all faded out.

It's time to drag myself up and go inside and call Daddy. He used to at least come home early every morning to say hi and change into some clean clothes to wear to work, but lately he's been keeping most of his things over at Janet's. I guess he figures why not? Pretty soon he'll be living there full-time. I know if I was him I'd stay home this week with me and Claude; I'd treasure these last days when it's just the three of us together. But Daddy's not very emotional. Family events kind of pass right over him. That's why I don't have to be all that careful about hurting his feelings like I do with Claude.

The house feels cool as I step inside and head toward the back hallway. It's very quiet. Claude's deep in dreamland. He'll probably stay that way half the day.

I pick up the phone and dial Janet's number. As usual, one of the boys answers. It's Petey. "Let me talk to Daddy," I say in a voice that means don't screw around with me, Petey, or I'll tear your head off.

"How come you call every morning?"

"Let me talk to Daddy!" I yell. It ruins my throat talking to those boys.

"Okay! Dean!" I hate the way Petey and Buster call Daddy "Dean."

I'm trying to think of what to say to Daddy when he answers. "Hi, darlin'."

"Hi."

"What's up?"

"Not much."

"What can I do for you?"

"Nothing much. I just wanted to talk."

"Well, that's good. But I have to hurry out of here on account of I'm already late for work." When I don't say anything, he goes on. "What are you planning to do today?"

"Nothing."

"Then how about you and Claude doing a little work? I'd really like the two of you to go to the store and get some big boxes and start putting your things in them. We've only got a week."

"When are you coming home again?" I ask, ignoring his request.

"I'll be home after work, so you all get busy, hear?"

"Daddy—"

"What?"

"I'm more convinced than ever that Claude is making a big mistake—"

He sighs.

"No, listen." I sit down in a chair, ready to have a real talk. "I really don't think he belongs in the military. He's not the type. Can you picture him marching or learning to shoot or—"

"Honey," Daddy interrupts me, "I've told you before —it's none of our business what Claude wants to do. If going in the Army is what he wants, then let him do it."

"But I'm not so sure that's what he really wants—I have a feeling he's just doing it on account of the mess his personal life's in. I think maybe his heart got broken."

Daddy sighs again. "Well, let's not worry about it, okay? Each of us has enough to do worrying about our own selves, don't you think?"

I don't know if Daddy even realizes that Claude and Marlene have broken up—he's not been around enough lately to notice, probably, but just as I open my mouth to tell him, he says, "Here, honey, Janet wants to talk to you. I've got to go. I'll see you when I get home."

"Dad—" But he's gone—and damn if he hasn't turned me right over to Janet!

"Morning, sunshine," she says. "How are you today?"

I close like a clam. I can just see her: soft white skin and dyed red hair. I can't believe Daddy finds that combination sexy.

"Fine." My voice is barely audible. "Can I talk to Daddy again, please?"

"He's already out the door, hon. He was late for work. I will be too, if I don't run," she says, though not in an unfriendly way.

"Then run." This mean manner just takes over me whenever I talk to Janet. "Go on—go," I say.

"Hon—" She pauses, probably trying to remember some article she read in *Redbook* about how to handle your stepdaughter. Janet's always trying to say the right thing, but I can just sense the hatefulness she feels for me underneath. "Maybe we can have a talk later," she says after a moment. "Just the two of us."

God, that's the last thing I want to do.

"I'd like to share some of my thoughts with you sometime," she says.

"Like what?"

"We don't have time to go into it all right now. But

I feel that you feel angry at me because Dean's been spending the night here so much lately. Now, you know you're welcome to start sleeping over here yourself, but —but you said you wanted to be at home with Claude—"

"I don't care if Daddy sleeps with you," I say.

"Oh. Well—" She laughs a little nervous laugh. "We'll have a talk soon. Okay?"

"I don't know. Maybe," I mumble.

But that doesn't seem to discourage her. "Good. Let's plan to do it, then," she says. "I better run now. 'Bye."

It's the middle of the afternoon and I'm watching one of my soaps when I hear Frances Pepper calling me from outside. Frances is my next-door neighbor and my only friend—I'm not interested in having a lot of friends.

"Bailey!" she yells. She's been instructed to always shout for me from our yard because I don't want her coming up on our porch and knocking on the door. And I don't want her coming into our house. I guess I like keeping my home life private.

I go to the window and look out at her. Frances just recently turned eleven, but she acts more like she's sixteen. She's standing in the middle of our yard now trying to twirl her baton. Her greatest desire in life is to be a member of Dancing Boots, the high school majorette team. She's been trying to learn to twirl for a couple of months. "What do you want?" I yell.

"Can you come out?" she asks, as she drops her baton for the hundredth time.

"What for?" I ask.

"Let's walk to Kmart," she says.

"It's too hot."

"No it's not."

"What are you going there for?"

"I need some earrings."

"You've already got a ton of cheap earrings in your jewelry box."

"I want some more. Come on."

I sigh. "Okay—lemme change."

As I go to my room to get one of my fishing caps, I wonder what I'll learn from Frances today. She's younger than I am, but she seems to know more about the facts of life than I imagine lots of grown-ups do. Believe it or not, she's the one who finally explained to me about periods. She also told me—in detail—what Danny Rubio and Christy Martin did that made Christy's parents send her to live with her aunt. And it wasn't just going all the way either. It was more than that. I found it unbelievable at the time, but then Frances showed me some dirty magazines that belong to her father, and now I'll believe anything. "If you can think of it, then someone, somewhere is doing it"—that's Frances's philosophy. We've tried to think of the most unbelievable, outrageous stuff to test that theory. You wouldn't believe some of the disgusting things we've come up with. But according to her, someone somewhere's doing them.

Frances tries to twirl her baton above her head as we walk along the scorching path that leads to the shopping center. I wish she'd just give up—it's too hot to keep dropping it and picking it up. It's too hot to even be outside—I'm about to die. "When are you moving?" she asks me.

"Next Tuesday. The day after the wedding."

"You going to be in the ceremony?"

"Heck no."

"How come?"

"They're just getting married at Janet's sister's, without any big ceremony or anything. But I wouldn't be in it even if they were having a big wedding."

"How come? Wouldn't they let you?"

"I don't know if they would or not. But if they did, I'd refuse. I don't approve of them getting married."

"When's Claude leaving?"

"Day after the wedding. On Tuesday."

"Really? *That* soon?"

Frances makes me sick sometimes, trying to talk like a grown woman. "Really? *That* soon?" I mimic her. "Yes, *that* soon! *That* soon! What do you want me to do about it?"

"What's wrong with you?" she asks.

"What's wrong with you?" I repeat.

She doesn't say anything else and neither do I. I'm too hot to bother.

Frances is a good sport, though. Even though I acted ugly, she tries to cheer me up when we get to Kmart. She hurries to the jewelry counter and exclaims, "Oh, come look! Try these on!" And she hands me a pair of giant pink plastic earrings.

I try them on. They look pretty good, but I give them back to her. "I can't wear cheap earrings. They make my lobes itch."

"Not mine," she says, putting them on.

"I know." Frances has no trouble wearing cheap stuff. She can wear cheap shoes too, because her feet are fat.

Frances buys the pink earrings for herself, and we go outside and sit on a bench near the parking lot. This is that time of day I hate the most. It's when dogs are most likely to die if you leave them in a parked car with all the windows rolled up. I look around to see if I can see any. I'd like to rescue one and have the owner arrested.

"I know what we can do," Frances says.

"What?"

"Rate butts."

"What?"

"When I visited my boy cousins in Tampa, they said they like to look at girls' butts and rate them on a scale from one to ten. Let's try it with all the boys we see."

We try rating butts for a while, but I get bored. Most of the boys we see are scrawny and uninteresting.

"Look, there's Marlene McKinney!" Frances says suddenly.

"Where?" I ask, jumping up.

Marlene is driving by in her Volkswagen bug. I figure she must be on her way next door to the Super-Drug, where she works as a cashier. "Marlene!" I shout, waving. But she doesn't seem to hear me as she drives on.

"Are Claude and her still broken up?" Frances asks.

"Yeah," I say, sitting back down.

"How come? Who broke up with who?"

"He broke up with her as far as I can tell. I don't know what happened. He won't talk about it."

"Do you like her?"

"Yeah. I love her. We were real close."

"What's she like? She seems like sort of a flirt."

"No, she's not. She's just real friendly. She used to help me shop for clothes, and she gave me lots of advice."

"What kinds of advice?"

"Just about boys and stuff."

"Yeah? What'd she say about them?"

"Oh, she told me to be friendly, try to be myself and act natural—so they don't just see me as a sex object." Actually I never thought that I was in much danger of becoming a sex object. I'm about as short as a nine-year-old, and my hair's usually so messy that Claude says I look like a wild child. But Marlene seemed to think I needed her advice, so maybe she knows something I don't.

"Guess what," Frances says after a moment.

"What?"

"Claude and Marlene were doing it."

I'm not sure I want to hear this. "Doing what?"

"Guess," she says sarcastically.

"How do you know?"

She gives me a look. She doesn't know. She's just trying to trick me so I'll tell her if I know different—or that I know the same. "You're wrong," I say. But I'm wondering now, *were* they doing it? I can't believe that it's never occurred to me before that Claude and Marlene might have been doing it. But now looking at the world through Frances Pepper's eyes, I'm thinking she's probably right—they were doing it.

"I'm burning up," Frances says after a while.

"Me too. Listen, I've got to get some boxes to take home. You want to stop at the Super-Drug with me and get them from Marlene?"

"Okay!"

When the Super-Drug's automatic doors swing open,
Frances and I get a blast of relief from the icy air-
conditioning. Marlene's already working at her register:
her freckled skin looks sunburned next to her white
uniform, and she's hugging her thin arms as she chats
with some cute guy.

I tell Frances to wait, and then I slip up behind Marlene and yank the back of her hair.

"Oh!" she squeals, and whirls around. "Oh, it's you!
I'll kill you, Bill!" she says, laughing as she pulls my
fishing cap off.

I laugh too. Marlene once invented all these funny
nicknames for my family—she calls me "Bill" for Bill
Bailey, and she calls Daddy "Mr. E." for Mr. Evans—
and get this, my favorite—she named Claude "Munchkin"! Picture calling a person six feet five inches
"Munchkin."

"What are you two up to?" she asks me and Frances.

"Just messing around. Frances bought some earrings."

Frances points to her ears.

"Oh, those are wild," Marlene says. "They look good
on you."

Frances just sort of smiles. I think she's nervous
being in Marlene's company. For all her talk, she doesn't
know that many older teenagers. She tries to do a little
twirl with her baton, but she drops it, of course.

"Whoops!" Marlene says kindly, and then she turns
to me. "You're looking great, Bill," she says.

"Me?"

"Yes, adorable! I love your haircut."

"My haircut?" She's got to be kidding.

"Yes, it's very sexy."

Frances stares at my head as if she's trying to figure out what in the world Marlene's talking about. "Oh, dahling, please," I say in a silly deep voice to cover my embarrassment.

"You're going to knock them dead in a couple of years, Bill. Seriously," Marlene says.

"Oh, please—please, fans, enough," I say. I take my fishing cap back from her and put it on. "How's the job?"

"Boring. I wish I could leave. I hate being cooped up here." She brushes her hair back from her face, then says, "How's your lazy brother? What's he doing today?" She's trying to sound casual, but I don't think she feels casual—I notice her pretty green eyes dart around as if she's afraid someone will hear her asking about him.

I shrug and try to sound casual too. "Not much. Probably sleeping. Or messing around with his short-wave radio, trying to locate some weather disaster."

Marlene shakes her head and grins. She and I used to tease Claude a lot about his interest in storms and weather disasters.

"Claude and I went to the beach last night about eight o'clock, and we saw you," I tell her.

"You did?" Her face seems to get redder than it already is.

"Yeah. You looked like you were having a lot of fun."

"What was I doing?"

"Playing volleyball with a bunch of boys."

"It wasn't all that much fun."

"Oh, yeah?" I say teasingly.

"Why? What did Claude say? Did he think I was having fun?" She sounds defensive, as if we caught her doing something wrong.

"No, I didn't mean it that way—"

"Well, you can just tell him those boys were all just friends." She looks away from me.

"You work here every afternoon now?" I ask to change the subject.

"Yeah, the night shift. Weekends. I hate it." She still sounds disturbed.

"I bet." I step aside as a girl comes up and pays for a pack of mints, and then after her a man buys some shaving lotion and a *Playboy*. Frances has wandered over to the cosmetic counter and is sampling lipsticks on her wrists. I'm anxious to talk some more with Marlene, to clear up any misunderstanding she might have that I was down on her for playing volleyball with the boys. Heck, I'm glad she looked happy—I hate the way Claude's been acting about her lately. I just wish she'd tell me exactly what went on between the two of them, so I'd know why they're so sensitive about one another. But more people get in line at the register—plus Frances returns and announces she's ready to leave.

"Okay," I tell her, and then I step back over to Marlene as she staples a receipt to a bag. "Marlene, can I get some boxes from the back? I need them for packing."

"Sure, go ask for Arnie," she says.

Frances and I go back and Arnie gives us a couple of large empty ScotTowel boxes from the storeroom. By the time we get back to Marlene, she's got a whole line of customers. I wait by the register for a while, but she seems too busy to talk with me now. " 'Bye, Marlene, I've got to go," I say finally, touching her elbow. "I'll see you later—"

"Oh!" she says, looking at me as if she hadn't realized I was still here. " 'Bye, Bill. Come back soon and visit!"

"I will," I say, and I really mean it—I'm just crazy about Marlene.

Three

I never know what kind of car Daddy's going to be driving home. He owns a used car place and seems to get a big kick out of driving a different car home every day. Today he's behind the wheel of a blue Pinto. Frances and I are sitting on the curb with my two boxes as he pulls up and parks.

"Hi, booger," I say as he gets out of the car.

"Hey, is that nice?" he asks.

"Hi, Mr. Evans," Frances says. "Look what I bought today." She shakes her big earrings at him.

"Gracious," he says, "those are big earrings."

She grins at him. It's no secret Frances has been in love with Daddy for over a year. She's told me she loves Claude too. "You really like them?" she says.

"Yeah. They're real nice. Cute," he says. I think Frances makes him uncomfortable.

"Look what I got," I say, slapping one of my boxes.

"Good girl." He pats me on the head and heads up the walk.

"He's beautiful," Frances says to me.

"He's forty," I remind her.

"He looks like a movie star."

"Ha." I stand up. These days I hate wasting even a minute when I can be with Daddy and Claude—just the three of us together. "Well, I have to go in," I say. "I'll see you tomorrow—'bye."

Before Frances can even say good-bye, I grab my boxes and hurry up to the house.

The air conditioner's running in the living room, and Claude's lying on the couch reading *The Old Farmer's Almanac*. I sit on the floor and watch as Daddy brings a beer in from the kitchen and switches the TV channels. He gets *M*A*S*H*, then sits down in his big chair and rubs his eyes with the palm of his hand. He's got sweat all over his face, and his shirt is wet. "You're going to catch cold," I tell him. I like looking after him.

He takes a big sip of beer and says, "Ah!"

"It's so cold in here, and you're all wet—you're going to get a cold," I warn him.

"Then can you get me a clean shirt, honey, please?"

"Sure!" I scramble up and go to his room. He doesn't have very many shirts left in his drawers because he's taken about all of them over to Janet's, but I dig under a pile of old socks till I find a tattered white undershirt. At least it's clean.

"Thanks," he says when he takes it from me.

I plop down again on the floor and watch him change. His belly hangs over his belt, but other than that he *is* fairly good-looking. He has blond curly hair and nice features—light-blue eyes. He catches me looking at him and smiles. I smile back, and then I sort of lean against the couch and tickle Claude's bare feet and go, "Whoo— whoo—whoo."

Claude doesn't look up from his *Almanac*, but he reaches out with one long foot and nuzzles my head with it. I look from Claude to Daddy—I just love looking at them both, one reading and the other watching TV. We're such a different family from Janet's. She's real normal and cheerful and positive, and her boys are so self-confident; whereas me and Claude—and Mom too— are moody, and we have odd interests and strange senses of humor. Daddy's always been somewhere in between. He seems to blow where the wind blows. I've seen him be dark and moody in the past, but lately he's been blowing Janet's cheerful way.

After a while the three of us migrate back to the kitchen and get busy making our own dinners. Daddy gets an open can of pork 'n' beans from the refrigerator. "You want some?" he asks me, spooning the beans into a saucepan.

"Yuk! No! Get that away from me," I say as I cut the crusts off my bread.

Claude laughs. "Offer her some S-P-A-M, Dad," he says, knowing just what I'll do—it's an old family joke.

Daddy smiles. "Want some Spam, Bailey?" he says.

"Oh no! Oh, God! *Help!*" I collapse against the counter and sink to the floor. I take a long time gagging and dying with my hands around my throat as Daddy and Claude laugh.

The next morning, as soon as I wake up, I head straight for Daddy's room. Just as I expected: His bed looks exactly the way it did yesterday. He must have slipped over to Janet's house after I went to sleep. You would think he could stay with me and Claude for just one lousy night. I hurry to the phone and dial Janet's number. Buster answers the phone. "Give me Dean," I say.

"Dean? Why are you—"

"Just give me Dean, you hideous little crapfish!"

Buster makes a rude sound into the receiver and then drops it. It seems like years before Daddy picks up the phone. "Hey," he says.

"Hey. How come you snuck away last night, Dean?"

"Bailey? What's going on—how come you're calling me Dean?"

"You let Petey and Buster call you Dean."

"Well, I'm not their daddy."

I'm glad to hear him say that at least. "Daddy, guess what."

"What?"

"Today's the first day of the rest of your life!" I laugh loudly. That's one of the dumb sayings Janet's got stuck on the refrigerator in her kitchen.

"Sorry, honey, but I don't have time to fool around. I'm late."

"You're always late. You all stay in bed too long."

"Hey—"

"Just kidding. I didn't mean anything funny."

"Honey, I can't talk now. I've got a busy morning ahead of me."

"Well, don't forget—if life gives you a lemon, make lemonade!" I laugh loudly again—this is another dumb saying Janet's got on her fridge.

"Okay, okay, Bailey. I'm hanging up now," Daddy says.

"Who's stopping you? Don't worry about me. I enjoy being an orphan."

"Good Lord. Would you stop all that now? You're acting crazy."

"No, I'm not. I just wonder why you can't stay under our roof for at least one night—can't you all ever be without each other?" I know I'm letting the devil get the best of me, but that doesn't seem to stop me.

Daddy doesn't say anything; I think I've embarrassed him.

"Well?" I ask.

"Hold on a second," he says, and I hear him talking with Janet in the background, but I can't make out what he's saying. A moment later he's back on the phone. "Listen, why don't you and I go to lunch together today? How about meeting me at Fat Man's Restaurant? Just the two of us."

"Seriously?"

"Yeah, I'm not joking. Meet me at noon, okay? Can you get there on your bike?"

"Yes sir."

"Okay, good. See you then."

"Okay. 'Bye, Daddy."

" 'Bye."

"Yippee," I say as I hang up the phone. I'm sure Janet put him up to this. But it's okay—it'll be nice to be alone with him for a change.

I look in on Claude on my way out of the house to meet Daddy. Lately Claude's been sleeping half the day. I guess it helps him escape all the things bothering him, like breaking up with Marlene, going to boot camp, leaving me. He's lying there perfectly still with the sheet pulled neatly up over his long body; when he sleeps, he doesn't wreck the bed at all—it stays as neat as a pin. His room's real neat too. He hasn't even begun to pack up his things: The Kmart painting he bought himself years ago is still hanging on the wall next to his bed. It's called *Autumn Leaves*. And on the desk there's his short-wave radio and his scrapbook with all the natural disasters in it. I wonder what will happen to Claude's things when he leaves for the Army. His tidy stack of *National Geographics*? His *Autumn Leaves* picture?

Isn't it funny—I mean the fact that Claude bought that oil painting? One day when he was about fourteen, right after our mother left, he went and bought it at Kmart for fifteen dollars and ninety-nine cents. It was like he wanted to start making a nice home for himself now that she was gone. I remember him carrying it along the highway with me following after him, and when we got home, he hung it in his room where he could see it from his bed. We don't have autumn leaves here in south Florida, so I guess it's a place he likes to visit in his mind. I don't blame him, really—it's very cozy-looking.

. . .

I get to Fat Man's before Daddy does, so I get us a booth by a window where I can watch for him. He finally drives up in a little Honda and I wave, but he doesn't see. When he walks in the door, he takes off his aviator sunglasses and squints around the room for me. I wave my fishing cap at him.

We both order the same thing—hamburgers and Cokes—and then Daddy excuses himself to go wash up. The waitress brings our Cokes while he's gone, and when he comes back and he's all set, he looks at me. "What are you grinning at, Miss Bubbly?"

"Frances says you look like a movie star."

"Good Lord." He makes an expression like I'm crazy.

"She's right. You do."

"Well, good. Now listen, honey—have you been feeling upset lately?"

"No."

"You sure? You've been worrying us a lot."

"Worrying who?"

"Me and Janet."

"Janet." I make a face. "You always talk about Janet."

"That's because I love her."

I suck my cheeks in and look away from him.

"Hey, now don't go looking away from me like that—"

I move my eyes to see him, but not my face. This must give me sort of a creepy sideways expression, because Daddy gets a little angry and says, "Now don't look at me like that! You've got to stop acting so nasty every time I mention Janet. That's one of the things I want to talk to you about."

I move my face around to look straight at him, but I keep sucking in my cheeks.

"Come on now, act your age."

I cross my eyes.

"Oh, Jesus," he says. "Why are you so ugly toward Janet?"

"She's ugly to me."

"She is not. She's an angel toward you."

"An angel?" I make a rude sound.

"Quit that!"

I look at him, surprised. It usually takes more than this to get Daddy going.

"Be nice," he says.

I hate it when he says dopey things like "Be nice." As far as I'm concerned, that's worse than yelling.

"I do not like Janet," I say as nicely as I can.

"*Why?*"

"She is a fake."

His face is getting red. The truth hurts. But I don't dare say that. I've got all my permanent teeth in. Ha. Really, Daddy wouldn't hit me; my mother's the only one who ever hit me.

"They say it's normal to not like your stepmother at first," he says. I guess Janet's been giving him some of her *Redbook* articles to read.

"Oh, yeah?" I ask. "Is it normal to hate her kids too?"

"Yeah. That's very normal."

"Is it normal to want to keep things the way they've been for the last few years?"

"Yeah, yeah. Probably."

"Is it normal to be so short for my age?"

He looks confused, and I can't help giggling. Sometimes he doesn't get my sense of humor. Claude always does, though. He would have laughed.

Daddy sighs and looks up. "Well, here comes our food. Let's try and enjoy it."

The waitress puts our hamburgers down and leaves. Daddy quickly lifts his top bun—he's checking to see if they remembered his onion. "Damn," he whispers, and he calls the waitress back and reminds her that he asked for onion. He waits silently for her to bring it to him on a little saucer, and then he gets busy eating. We don't talk while we eat.

When we're through, Daddy seems to feel more at ease. He picks his teeth with a toothpick and studies me. "So, what are you going to do today?" he says.

I shrug. "I'll probably see Frances."

"You do have some friends besides that little girl, don't you, honey?"

I drain the rest of my Coke through the straw, then look at him and say, "No."

His face falls. "How come?"

I shrug.

He sighs. "That's not normal," he says.

I can't help smiling. Here we go again. "It's not?"

"No."

"Is it normal to—"

"Okay, okay," he says, catching on, "Let's not go through that again."

I make a silly face, then chomp on some of the ice from my glass.

"You got anything else on your mind? Anything you want to discuss?" Daddy says.

"Yeah, I have a question about Claude."

"What is it?"

"I was just wondering what you and Janet were planning on doing with all his possessions."

"His possessions?"

"Yeah, his radio and pictures and all."

"I don't know. We haven't thought about it yet."

"You haven't even thought about it?" I ask slowly with astonishment.

"Oh, come on now. Let's not make a mountain out of a molehill."

"I'm not making a mountain out of a molehill. This is no molehill!"

"Calm down. What are you getting so worked up for?"

"Because of your lack of interest in Claude's things!"

"You worry about Claude too much."

"Well, someone has to worry about the children in this family!"

"We do. Plenty. Janet worries about you a lot."

"Janet. Janet. Janet. What about you?"

"Me too. I love you. And Janet loves you too."

"Oh, puke."

Daddy looks at me and rolls his toothpick from side to side with his tongue. "You've got a real bad attitude, you know that?" he says.

"I know she really hates me."

"Well, she probably should the way you've treated her. But she doesn't."

I lean forward. "She does. I know she'd like to kill me!" I grab his arm. "Save me, Daddy!" I say in this fake scared voice.

A couple of people look around at us, and Daddy gets real embarrassed. "Bailey, you're a damn nut!"

I burst out laughing and sit back. Daddy gets control of himself and just shakes his head. "This is serious," he says. "You are a case."

"You are too!" I'm sort of hoping he'll get worked up and yell again. But instead he just resumes gnawing on his toothpick. "Maybe you'd like to see a family counselor," he says after a moment.

"*No.* No. No. No. No. No. No . . ."

I'm still carrying on with the no's when he looks at his watch and reaches for the check. "Okay, okay, let's go. We'll never get anywhere this way." He rises to go as I keep saying, "No. No . . ." and I'm sliding down out of my seat till my butt's nearly touching the floor. I've regressed to being about six years old.

Daddy leaves me and walks over to the cash register, and I stand up, catch my breath, and put my fishing cap on. I *am* a nut, but I *know* it—and that makes all the difference in the world.

After Daddy pays, he beckons for me to come on. On the way out of the restaurant, he tries to put his arm around me, but I scoot away from him.

Four

I ride my bike home over the cracked sidewalk that runs along the highway, past yucca trees and sea grape plants. The reason I'm so worried about Claude's possessions is I'm afraid that someday soon I'm going to turn around and there'll be no trace of him left. His books, his desk, his brown-and-blue-striped bedspread—they'll all be gone, swallowed up the way our mother's things were. I have some little mementos of her, but nothing big, like her red quilted bathrobe or her Chinese silk jewelry box or this black bean-bag chair she loved. After she left, a friend of hers named Juanita came over and took all her stuff away. Daddy helped Juanita put Mom's things in the back of an old station wagon, and that's the last I ever saw of them. The few times I visited my mother, I didn't see any of the things I remembered. I didn't want to ask her about them, though, because I figured she might not know where they were either, and I didn't want to get her upset by making her remember them.

It's raining by the time I pedal up our street, and Marlene McKinney is running across our lawn toward her car. "Hey, Marlene!" I yell.

She stops and shelters her head with her hand and looks in my direction. "What are you doing? Did you visit with Claude?" I ask, wheeling my bike across the wet grass.

"No! I came to see him, but he doesn't answer the door," she says as she squints against the raindrops.

"He's probably asleep. He sleeps real late, you know."

"Oh—right," she says, but I suspect that she suspects what I suspect: that Claude is up, but he's just not answering the door because he knows it's her.

"Well, I'll see you later," she says as she turns away from me and starts off.

" 'Bye—I'll come visit you at your store!" I shout.

I watch her run across the lawn. With her long legs and knobby knees, Marlene looks like an awkward colt when she runs. She ducks down and gets in her Volkswagen; then a moment later her wipers come on and she takes off.

I find Claude standing at the kitchen window watching the rain come down in our backyard. "Marlene was looking for you," I tell him.

He doesn't say anything.

"Didn't you hear her ring the doorbell?"

"Don't worry about it," he says sharply.

"I'm not worried." I'd like to tell him not to get mad

at me just because he's mad at Marlene. But I just stand there next to him watching out the window as the rain starts to come down harder. It's bending the branches of our umbrella trees and our little hibiscus tree. I'll miss these trees and I'll miss looking out the window at storms with Claude. I'd like to fall down at his feet right now and throw my arms around his legs and beg him not to go in the Army, scream at him and sob and sob.

He starts to walk away from the window.

"Hey," I say.

He stops. "What?"

"I bet you're going to run into all kinds of interesting weather when you're in the Army. What do you think?"

He shrugs.

"They'll probably make you march in weather like this—or when it's twenty below zero. I wouldn't be surprised."

"Cut it out," he says.

"Cut what out? I didn't do anything wrong."

"Quit trying to turn me against the Army. I'm going whether anyone else likes it or not—"

"I'm not trying to turn you against the Army!" I yell, stung.

"Yes you are."

"I am not! I want you to go into the Army! I hope you have a *fabulous* time in the Army! A *wonderful*—"

"Oh, shut up," he says, and he starts out of the kitchen.

"Hey! You just shut up!" I yell. Why's he being so mean to me?

"Drop dead" is the last thing I hear before he leaves the room.

"You drop dead! You donkey-dip doo-doo!" I take off

after him, but he hurries to his room and closes his door, and by the time I get there, it's locked. I kick the door and yell, "Open up, greaseball!"

"Go away, Bailey!"

"No!" I yell, beating my fists on his door. "I don't care if you go in the Army! I don't care about your stupid love life, and I don't care about your stupid possessions either! What are you going to do about them, anyway?" I bang on his door again. "What? Answer me! You planning on just leaving them here? We're moving, remember! We won't have room for your things at our new house! You want me to burn your stuff? I'll burn it—or I'll give it to Petey and Buster and they'll mutilate it! How about that? They'll destroy your *Autumn Leaves* picture, Claude!" I sink down to the floor and flop my hands down on either side of me. "Hey—what possessed you to buy that dumb picture anyway?" I hoot loudly. "You're crazy, Claude, you know that? I don't care what happens to you or your old stuff. It's stupid stuff—I hate it. Why are you leaving, anyway? You want to die and get tortured by some enemy?" I whoop again. "Ha! I hope you do! I hope they torture you and tear you apart. I don't care about you."

I press my ear to his door. I can hear him playing his shortwave radio. "Hey!" I beat my fist against the wood. "Hey! You're weird! You know that? Everybody's going to make fun of you in the Army! You're going to be the tallest, weirdest one!" I laugh a little more.

Finally I drag myself up and kick his door one more time before wandering into my room and throwing myself down on my bed, exhausted.

. . .

When Daddy comes home, I don't hurry out of my room
to greet him as usual. I hate both him and Claude right
now. I might not be able to stop the two of them from
deserting me, but I'm not going to be nice and agreeable
about it either. There's a tap on my door. "Bailey?"
Daddy says. "Darlin'?" It's hard to resist answering
when he sounds so sweet, but I succeed. "Claude says
you've been having a fit," he says.

"*A fit*," I mimic silently.

"Hey—are you in there?" Daddy says after a moment.

"Yeah," I say, just to keep his interest up.

"Can I come in?"

"I don't care."

He opens my door. But I don't look up from one of
Janet's old *Redbook*s I'm pretending to read.

"What's happening to you?" he says.

I just shrug, keeping my eyes glued to the magazine.

"You don't want to talk about it?" he says.

I shrug again, hoping he'll press harder, maybe even
come sit beside me.

But instead he sighs and says, "Okay, have it your
way," and then he leaves and closes my door.

"Leave me alone!" I shriek, furious because he's doing
just that.

Later I don't go in the kitchen to cook with the two
of them. I picture them in there missing me while they
fix their dinners. They're used to me keeping their spirits
up, making jokes and teasing them both—that's why
Daddy calls me Miss Bubbly sometimes. I get the idea in
my head that they're really upset because I'm staying
in my room. But when I crack my door and peer down the
hall, I hear them talking in the kitchen like normal—

they don't sound sad at all. "Shut up!" I scream and slam my door. And neither of them even comes to check and see whether I've completely lost my mind.

Night takes forever. Ordinarily I'd sit up late watching TV with Claude, but being mad at him makes me stay in my room. Being mad at him also makes me decide to make a phone call. You'll never guess who I call. My mother. Claude hates it when I call her—he says it's better if we just pretend she's dead. Let him think that way. I don't have to. He's always trying to get me to turn against her. He doesn't give her a chance; he doesn't remember how great she can be—like the time she took me to the Seaquarium on Key Biscayne a couple of years ago. We ate ice cream as we watched the diver in the giant fish tank feed all these fish—including the biggest turtle I've ever seen in my life; to this day I can hardly believe the size of that turtle. And Mom took off her new brown high-heeled shoes because they hurt her feet, and I took off my sandals to be like her, and we held our shoes as we walked over this little wooden pathway that led from the manatee exhibit to the killer whale pool.

I carry the phone from the hallway into my room, and after I shut the door, I dial my mother's number long distance. She lives a couple of hours away in Miami.

The phone rings about ten times before I finally hang up and lie back on my bed. She's probably out somewhere with her boyfriend, Charlie. They've been living together for almost two years. I never liked Charlie very much, except the last time I talked to Mom, she told me he'd given up drinking, so at least I like him for that. I'm hoping he might help her quit. My mother can be so great when she's not drinking—like that day at the Seaquarium. I remember she was wearing a tight brown dress, and she smelled of perfume and had on lots of green eye shadow. She was polite to me all day. She spoke softly and put her hand against my hair several times, remarking on how fine my hair was, like silk, she said. She stroked my face, and later when she put me on the bus to go back home, she had tears in her eyes. That was a golden day as far as I was concerned. But the next time I called her, she acted as if she only half remembered that I'd even been to see her. I reminded her of the new shoes she'd taken off and held as we'd walked around, and she said, "What new shoes?" "Those brown high-heeled shoes!" I screamed, and she screamed back at me to leave her alone.

I get restless thinking about all this, so I jump up and go out into the living room. Claude's watching TV, but Daddy's not there—I guess he's already left for Janet's. I sit in a chair in the corner, making an effort not to look at Claude. But at one point I glance at him and he simultaneously looks over at me. Before he can say anything, I jump up and go back to my room.

The next morning as soon as I get up, I call Daddy over at Janet's. When Petey answers, I say in a deep voice, "Is Mr. Evans there?"

"Who is this?" Petey asks. I know he suspects it's me, but I've never asked for "Mr. Evans" before, so he's not sure.

"It's Bonnie, his secretary."

"It's not Bailey?"

"Pardon?"

"Wait," he says, and he goes to get Daddy. Petey knows I'd never say "Pardon."

"Hey, Bon, what's up?" Daddy says a minute later.

I don't say anything.

"Bonnie?"

"It's not Bonnie," I say in a singsong voice.

"Oh. Hi, Bailey." He sounds a little perturbed. Well, I'm perturbed too. In fact, the only reason I'm calling is to show him I'm not speaking to him. "What's up?" he asks.

I don't say anything.

"Bailey?"

Nothing. Not a word.

"Why did you call?"

I don't answer.

"Oh, boy," he sighs. "Let's have this talk later, honey. I don't have time now."

Talk? He thinks we're having a talk.

"Honey, I have to go now. I've got a customer coming early. Wait—what?" he asks Janet in the background. "Oh, yeah," he says back to me. "Janet wants you and Claude to meet all of us at Spanish River Park after work today around seven. We're going to have a cookout."

Oh, brother.

"Tell Claude, now, and we'll see you both then." He hangs up before even giving me the chance to not say good-bye.

When Claude gets up around one o'clock, I don't say, "How did you sleep?" or "It's about time!" like I normally would. Instead I ignore him when he comes in the living room, and when he sits on the couch and starts watching my soap with me, I get up and carry my bowl of Cocoa Puffs across to the TV set and sit down right in front of it.

"Can you move, please?" he says.

I shift a little.

"I still can't see," he says.

I shift a little more.

"Thanks," he says. "What's happening with Devon and Clarence? Why's he being so mean to her?"

It's hard for me not to answer; I enjoy filling Claude in on my soaps, but I act as if I don't hear him.

"Oh, you're not speaking, is that it?" he says.

"I'm speaking." I take another bite of cereal and look back at him. "I called Mom last night." He stares at me for a moment, then looks back at the TV. "Don't worry —she wasn't home."

He doesn't say anything.

"It's okay if I call her," I say.

He still doesn't say anything.

Claude and I have had a running argument for the last few years: I say we forced Mom to leave, and he says she left on her own. The facts are that Daddy and a social worker took her to an alcoholic rehabilitation center, and when she quit the program there, Daddy refused to let her come back home. Claude admits that's true, but says she didn't put up much of a fight. He says she chose drinking over us.

But he's not saying anything now; he's just staring woodenly at the TV. I have a feeling the discussion is closed.

"Janet invited us to a cookout today at Spanish River Park. It's at seven o'clock," I say.

"Good," he says with a little nod of his head.

"You're going?" I ask.

"Sure, aren't you?"

"No way."

"Oh, Bailey, for God's sake. Why don't you give Janet a break for a change?"

"Because she makes me sick!"

"Well, you're crazy. She's good for you. When are you going to get it through your dumb head that some people are good for you and some people are bad for you? Janet can help you grow up! Mom would've just killed you!"

"You're crazy," I say, spilling the milk out of my bowl as I slam it down on the floor. "You're about as crazy as they come." I jump up and head for the front door.

"Run from the truth," he yells.

"Shut up!" I slam the door and go out onto the porch and just stand there barefoot on the scorched wooden floor, hugging myself and hating all the dumb idiot people in my life. Every stupid one of them.

"Bailey!" It's Frances calling from next door.

"What do you want?" I yell crossly.

She just waves as she heads over to my porch in her little yellow halter top and short shorts. "Hey," she says.

"Hey yourself. Don't come up on my porch."

"Don't worry, I don't want to come up on your porch." Frances is amazingly tolerant sometimes. If I were her, I'd tell me to go to hell. "What are you doing?" she asks.

"Nothing."

Neither of us says anything until I sense she might be about to leave; then I say quickly: "How would you feel if first your mother left, and then your father went and joined another family, and then your only brother left you to join the Army?"

She just stares at me and shrugs.

"Well, would you like it or not?" I ask her.

"Aren't you going with your dad?" she says.

"I'm supposed to, but I don't want to."

"Why not?"

"He's marrying a witch. Everyone thinks she's so nice, but I know she'd claw me to death if I gave her half a chance."

"Why don't you go live with your mother?" she says.

"Because she's an alcoholic."

"Really?"

"Sure."

"What did she do?" Frances makes a face as if she's expecting to hear the worst. I've never told her any of this—she moved next door after Mom left.

"She was a wreck. She drank or slept all the time— till Daddy and this social worker forced her to go into an institution. She never came home after that."

Frances looks stunned. "When she left, did you miss her?" she asks.

I laugh. "Yeah—like I'd miss a hole in the head." This isn't true. But I guess I feel sort of puffed up from presenting Frances with some of my own shocking facts of life. Really I did miss my mother. I missed her for a long time.

Five

At seven Claude leaves to meet Janet and Daddy and the boys at Spanish River Park. I know I told him I wasn't going, but as soon as his car's gone, I get my bike and beat it over there.

I park near the entrance gate and walk slowly around a little lake toward the picnic area until I can see them all in the distance. Their little group seems to be having a ball: Petey and Buster are splashing each other under an outdoor shower, and Janet and Claude are talking and laughing while Daddy's starting a fire on the grill. The sun's filtering down through the trees, making giant shadows everywhere, and a couple of snow-white egrets are strutting on top of an empty picnic table nearby. As I watch the smoke rising from the grill, and I watch Claude snapping open a can of soda, I start losing some of my resolve not to be with all of them. Besides being hungry and thirsty, I don't particularly want to go back home and be by myself.

A strong breeze suddenly shakes all the trees, making the shadows shift and squirrels scamper over the ground. Daddy points to a couple of raccoons lumbering up from the lake, and Claude gets up and tries to shoo them off. I don't blame him—raccoons will take the food right off your table if you let them. Claude seems to be having a silly conversation with the raccoons. At least he's making Daddy and Janet laugh. I wish I could hear what he's saying. Before I even realize it, I'm walking toward everybody; and before I can come to my senses, Janet spots me. "Oh boy! Look who's here!" she says. "I'm glad you changed your mind!"

Daddy looks around and sees me and grins. "Hey, good," he says.

I glance at Claude as I sit down at the picnic table. He grins at me, but I just scowl back and look away. I don't want him to think I've gotten over being mad with everybody.

"We are so glad you came!" Janet says, and she walks over and pats my head.

All right—enough. I sort of duck down to discourage her from touching me as I stare at the raccoons lumbering back toward the lake; I'd be just as happy now if all the attention would leave me.

"Claude, can you do me a favor and get the chips and Doritos out of that grocery bag?" Janet says. "I'll serve up the potato salad."

Claude puts the potato chips on the table, and I rip

open the bag and start stuffing them in my mouth as I watch Janet getting the potato salad out of her Styrofoam cooler. She's wearing a pair of green shorts with a pink polo shirt—not very good colors for a redhead, I think. And look at that—her hair doesn't even move when she bends her head over the cooler. Doesn't she know that hair spray's old-fashioned?

Janet catches me staring at her and gives me a quick wink. Then she comes over to the table and opens the potato-salad carton and starts dishing the stuff out. I don't take my eyes off her. When she gets to my plate, I flatten my hand over it and say, "None for me."

"You don't want any?"

"I hate potato salad. So does Daddy. Don't give him any either." I slide my hand over Daddy's plate too.

"Oh, I thought he liked it," Janet says.

I shake my head. "He hates it like I do."

"Really?"

"Sure, just ask him."

She sighs as she looks away from me. "Sweetie? Dean?"

"What?" Daddy says.

"You want some potato salad?"

"Sure."

"I thought you hated potato salad!" I yell.

"No, it's okay," he says.

"He used to hate it," I say to Janet.

"Well, you never can tell with men," she says.

I glare at her and move my hand away, and she puts some potato salad on his plate. She doesn't give him much, though—just a teeny plop—so I guess I half win.

"Okay, we're ready to eat," she says, sounding relieved. "Come, boys! Pronto! Pronto! We're going to eat, eat, eat!"

I go back to my potato chips as Petey and Buster charge over from the shower, wet and trembling. They look like bald little birds with their backbones and ribs sticking out and their skinny limbs. And their hair's cut real short—they got it cut that way so they'd look like Army men. "Hey, what's she doing here?" Buster yells when he sees me.

"Shut up," I tell him as I chomp on some chips.

"Give me a potato chip," he says.

"No!" I lift the bag out of his reach.

"Gimme. Please."

"No."

"They're not yours. Mom, tell her to give me a potato chip."

"Relax, Buster," Claude says. "Bailey, give him a potato chip."

"In a minute," I say.

"Mom," Buster whines, "tell her—"

I squeal suddenly as Petey's hand comes over my shoulder and grabs the potato-chip bag. He's climbed up on the bench behind me. I wrestle the bag back from him. "Don't!" I yell.

"Stop it!" Janet says. "Both of you! Please. Please. Let's take the chips away for now." She reaches out her hand toward me. "Please, Bailey—"

"C'mon, Bailey," Claude says.

"Shut up," I tell him, but I thrust the bag at Janet.

"Get down now, Petey, sit. Pronto, Petey!" Janet says. By now he's picking at the potato salad with his fingers.

"Get down!" I yell at him. I'd like to push him right off the bench.

"Okay! Okay!" Janet says. "Stop! Everyone! Bailey, why don't you get some sodas from the cooler? The boys will take the grape ones, and give me and Dean a Tab."

"Get the sodas," Claude says, nudging me when he sees I'm about to protest.

I sigh and drag myself up from the table, thinking I'm not Janet's slave, and since when does *Dean* drink Tab? He used to hate Tab too.

When I get back to the table, Janet's still telling Petey to sit down. She swats at his behind—but that only makes him giggle and stamp his feet. "Okay, you won't get a weenie if you act this way," Janet says to him.

Oh, *please*—a "weenie"? That's obscene.

Meanwhile Buster's hopping around Daddy with a paper plate in his hands, proclaiming that he wants another weenie. He's wolfed down the first one Daddy gave him in about two seconds flat.

"You'll have to wait, son, until everybody gets one," Daddy says patiently. It makes me sick that he's always nicer to those boys than he should be.

"No!" Buster says, grinning over at me. "Give me Bailey's!"

I start to stand up.

"Come on, Buster," Claude says sharply. I think he senses danger.

"Here—take this to Mama," Daddy says, putting a dog on Buster's paper plate.

"No—I want it."

"Give it to Janet, Buster," Daddy says.

Buster does what Daddy says, finally, and goes and

puts the hot dog on the picnic table. When he returns with another paper plate, Daddy gives him another dog and says, "Now take this to Bailey."

Buster grins at me as he starts to head over to the table, and then—accidently on purpose—he trips and my hot dog rolls right over the edge of the paper plate and falls into the sand. "Whoops," he says.

In a flash I'm up—and I grab him and I grab the hot dog from the sand and I beat it against his little shaved head. Buster squeals until Daddy jerks me off of him.

"It was an accident!" Buster yells.

"It wasn't!" I yell back.

Daddy grabs me and shakes me. "Stop it, young lady!" he says. "Now you just stop it—I mean it!"

"Let go!" I yell.

He shakes me again. "Don't you yell at me! What's wrong with you? Janet went to all this trouble and you just try and wreck it! I wish she hadn't invited you!"

I break loose from his grasp and start walking away from the group.

"Bailey—" Claude calls.

But I just keep going, scaring the raccoons near the lake as I rush past them. One of them jumps back, but then reaches out his stupid paw, begging for food. "Get out of here," I growl. "Go drown yourself!"

I hate Daddy's guts for yelling at me in front of those boys. "I wish you didn't invite me too!" I shout as I ride my bike home. "I'm not a member of your stupid family!"

I don't have a family anymore—I feel like I got caught in some crack between our old family and Daddy's new family and now I've got no family.

I'm still mumbling as I throw my bike down on the grass and head up to our porch. "Eat dirt, Buster. You too, Petey—"

When I get inside, I punch the air in the shadowy living room, then finally collapse onto the couch, worn out. I start thinking about my mother as I stare out the window at the twilight sky. I picture her and Charlie having dinner right about now, a nice peaceful dinner without any bratty little kids around. I sort of wish I was eating with them. You know, if my mother stopped drinking like Charlie has, I could possibly enjoy living with the two of them—be a member of their family.

I get up and go into the dark hall and pick up the receiver and dial Mom's number. When she answers, my heart skips a beat.

"Mom?"

"Who is this?"

"Bailey."

"Oh, hi, Bailey."

"Hi, Mom. How are you?"

"Okay. How are you?"

"Oh, I'm mad at everybody." I laugh a little, then wait for her to say something, but she doesn't. So I go on, "What have you been up to lately?"

"Oh. Nothing. Working . . ."

Is she going to say anything else? I help her out. "Has your health been good?"

"No," she says. "It's not good."

"How's Charlie?"

"He's gone."

"Where did he go?"

"His mother's."

"In Delray?"

"Yes."

"For how long? Did he go on a visit?"

She doesn't answer for what seems like a long time; then she finally says, "No, he left for good."

"You mean you two broke up?"

"Yeah, I guess."

I feel kind of sick. I hate picturing her all alone. Charlie must have given up on her like Daddy did.

"Are you okay?" I ask.

"Yeah, I'm okay." She sounds bored.

"There's no other news?"

"No."

"Oh."

She doesn't say anything for a long moment. Finally I say, "Well, I guess I'll talk to you later."

"Thanks for calling," she says.

"You're welcome."

"Come see me."

"I will. Maybe we could go to the Seaquarium again."

She doesn't answer.

"Mom?"

"What?"

"Never mind. 'Bye, Mom."

" 'Bye."

We hang up, and I just stand frozen in the dark hall

for a minute. Of course, I can't go see her—I don't have any way to get there. Claude and Daddy won't take me. I've taken a Trailways a few times by myself to Miami; but last December when I made the trip, an old man exposed himself to me in the station, so I vowed never to go on the bus again.

I go back into the living room and sit on the sofa and look out the window. My mother's all alone again. I feel like my mother's more alone than anyone on earth. I picture her sitting at her kitchen table looking out at this same twilight sky, drinking alone.

Do you know, I've never even been drunk? I don't have any idea what it's like. Here drinking's been my mother's most favorite thing and I don't even know why she likes it—why she chose it over our family.

I get up from the sofa and head back to the kitchen. I move cautiously, as if some invisible eyes were watching me. I almost laugh at them. No one will find out, I'm thinking. I'll just drink a little from this old wine bottle I've seen a million times up in the cabinet over the refrigerator. It's some cheap kind of wine in a bottle shaped like a fish. A man gave it to Daddy as a joke. He called it rotgut—I guess because it rots your guts. I just hope Daddy hasn't already carted it over to Janet's.

No. He hasn't. Good. I get up on the counter and slip the heavy fish-shaped bottle off the shelf. The wine in it is cherry pink. I hop down onto the floor, cradling the bottle to my chest, and hurry into my room and shut the door. My room's such an incredible mess with so much junk on the floor that I have to take giant steps, as if I'm hopping from one pond rock to another to get across to my bed.

I giggle as I land on my bed; I'm already acting silly and I haven't even taken a sip. It's hard to screw the lid off the bottle, but after tapping it against the bedpost several times, I manage. Then I lean my head back and take a good swallow. God, it *is* disgusting! It is rotgut! I hold my nose and gag as I take a second swallow. I guess the only way to get this over as quick as possible is to guzzle it, so I lean my head back farther and glug about half of it down, then look up and go, "Aghhh!"

I don't feel a thing. I'm wondering if the effect of this stuff has died out since it's been on the shelf so long—or maybe it wasn't all that alcoholic to begin with, given that it's pink colored and the bottle is shaped like a fish. I glug down some more, then wait a minute.

I think I'm starting to feel something, but I can't say exactly what. I pick up a *Redbook* and thumb through it. I don't seem to be able to concentrate on any of the writing, and my heart's beating really fast—but I can't tell if all this is from the wine or just from the excitement I'm feeling.

After a couple more minutes I try to stand up. Before I know it, I slip and the bottle falls to the floor, and the rest of the rotgut starts spilling out over a bunch of my comics. I lunge for the bottle, but I fall instead, my arms and legs going in all directions. I reach for my comics to save them, but I'm so dizzy all I can do is clutch at them, tearing the pages as my chin bounces against the floor. Then I try to get up, clutching the drenched comics to my face, but I slip again, and this time I hit my head against the bed, and my cheek smacks against the grimy wet floor. At some point during all of this, I realize I'm not having much fun.

"Stand up," Claude's saying. "Come on, stand."

I can't answer him, but in a blur of sight and feeling I can tell he's pulling on my arms, trying to get me up off the floor.

"Good Lord, I don't believe this." I hear Daddy's voice.

I close my eyes again and try to turn away so both of them will leave me alone—everything is spinning around.

"Pick her up by the legs, Dad—"

My middle caves in as Claude gets me under the arms and Daddy gets my legs and they heave me up onto the bed, putting me down on top of a bunch of books and junk. I try to turn over again and close my eyes—I just want to die.

But the next thing I know one of them's wiping my face with a cold cloth. I groan and try to move away. Through the fog I hear Claude tell me to *quit moving.* So I give up and just make horrible faces while he wipes my forehead, and then I try to say I'm sick, and I turn my head and puke all over the floor. "Oh Lord," I hear— it must be Daddy. The next thing I know, I'm peeing and I can't stop myself from doing it—I'm getting my jeans all wet—and then everything starts disappearing again into a sickening, swirling kind of blackness.

It's morning. I feel hot and sick as I open my eyes and peer at the sunlight coming in through my venetian blinds, making shadow stripes across my wall. I'm in my nightgown. After I passed out last night, Daddy and

Claude must have cleaned me up and changed my clothes.

I turn my head slowly and stare with my eyes half closed at the floor. It's clean—they must have cleaned up the vomit too. And did I really pee on myself? I wonder. I pray that I just dreamed that I did that. Except I'm pretty sure I really did. God, I wish I could die. I wish I never had to see Daddy and Claude again, I'm so humiliated.

I also feel as if there's this giant clamp around my head and some hand is tightening it tighter and tighter, but I'm so weak and in so much pain, I can't move away or make the hand quit. And I feel like I might have to throw up again. My mouth tastes like the inside of an old tennis shoe, one that's just been worn in a twenty-mile race.

My mother gave up our family for *this*? She *chose* to feel like this? I'm sure I've never felt this bad before in my whole life. No one would really choose this. I'm sure of that now. I imagine that some giant hand, like the one that's tightening the clamp around my skull now, some giant black-gloved hand must have kept pulling my mother down and wouldn't let her up. It kept pulling her down until all she could do in the end was to crawl away from us like some sick dog, leave so we wouldn't see her puking and crying anymore. That's exactly how I feel right now. I wish I could crawl away. I wish I never had to see Daddy and Claude again.

But Daddy comes into my room before the shadow stripes even leave my wall, and he's bringing a glass of orange juice with him.

I just groan when I see him standing over me. "Hey," he says.

"Hi."

"How are you?"

"Sick."

"I thought you would be. Want some of this?"

"Yes."

He helps support my head and tilts the juice glass back and I take a sip. His face is all clean-shaven, and his hair is wet and curly from his shower. "It's refreshing, isn't it?" he says.

"Yes." I take the glass from him and hold it with both hands as I drink some more. He sits down on the edge of my bed and stares at me. I feel my face getting red knowing that he must have helped clean me up and change my clothes last night. He doesn't seem all that embarrassed, though, sitting there looking at me. There are deep lines on his forehead and at the corners of his eyes. I never paid attention to his wrinkles before; he looks like he's getting kind of old.

I give him back the glass. "I'm sorry for what I did," I mumble. The clamp is so tight around my brain now that I grimace and close my eyes as I lean back to rest again.

"Well, why did you do that? Why'd you drink that stuff?"

I open my eyes again, but I'm too queasy to answer him.

"Did you do it because I got mad at you at the cookout?"

I shrug and nod at the same time.

"Well, you were being a real brat!"

Please, later. I wish he wouldn't talk now.

"You were asking for it, weren't you? Janet says you want my attention." He stands up and runs his hand through his hair. "Is that what it is? Do you want my attention?"

"No."

"Good. Because right now if you wanted my attention, I'd have to spank you. And I don't want to do that. So it's better if you don't get my attention now, isn't it?" He stands there with his arms crossed, staring at me, waiting for a response. But the top of my head feels like it's coming off, so I just close my eyes again.

"Bailey!"

"What?" I wish he wouldn't yell at me when I can't yell back or anything, when my head feels like this. We could have a good fight if I was well.

He sits down again on my bed and leans forward. "What am I going to do with you? Why did you get drunk? You want to act like your mother? You don't want to do that! Please, don't—don't do this again—" He sounds as if he's coming unglued.

I can't answer him—all I can do right now is grit my teeth to keep from throwing up.

"So what am I going to do with you?" he asks loudly.

"Kill me," I mutter.

"You want me to kill you?"

"Yes. Shoot me."

He pauses for a second, then says, "Well, no, I'm not going to shoot you."

"Why not?"

"Because you're my little girl. The only one I have."

There's a long silence between us as I stare at the stripes on my wall.

"You just lie here and rest today," he says after a while, patting my knee.

I don't plan to go dancing.

"Claude will get you anything you need," he says.

I nod, wishing he didn't have to leave right now.

"Well, 'bye." I hear his shoes crunch over my junk as he crosses my room. "I love you," he says.

I'd like to tell him I love him too, but before I can get my mouth to work, he's gone.

I'm almost asleep again when I hear, "Whoo—whoo."

I open my eyes just a little. The clamp s bearing down harder than ever. "Whoo—whoo." Claude's standing by my bed. His straight springy hair is falling down over his forehead as he grins at me. This is the first time *he's* ever pretended to be the ape. I'd like to laugh, but my face hurts too much to even smile.

"You need anything?" he says.

"No."

"Then go back to sleep."

"Okay." I close my eyes and try to do exactly that, figuring he'll leave my room. But when I open them again a moment later, I see him standing by my window, staring out. It's cloudy now, as if the sky's getting ready for our daily downpour. He looks pretty frail just standing there, so tall and thin in the dull light. I guess he wants to help me, but he doesn't know how. He's probably worried that I'm going to destroy myself after he leaves. He might be right. Something in me just seems to be forcing me to the brink these days. I'd like to tell him my new knowledge about Mom—about the giant hand pushing her down, over and over again. But I feel too sick now, and even if I could talk, I don't think I could make him understand.

Six

Janet calls me early the next morning. "Hi, hon," she says, "how are you feeling today?"

"Okay." I am better, but I still feel weak and light-headed from not eating for two days—I've probably lost about five pounds.

"Listen, I'm sorry you got so upset that you went and drank that wine. I'd like to talk with you about your feelings and all. Today, if that's possible."

Oh, brother.

"I was wondering if you could meet me on my lunch break. If you came by the office around noon, we could have about half an hour together."

I don't say anything.

"Will you, honey? Please?"

"Okay." I'm only doing it on account of Daddy. I'm afraid he'll hate me forever if I don't.

Brother, coming here was a huge mistake, I realize as I plop down on a leather chair in the gynecologist's office where Janet works. My extremities are about to freeze off in this air-conditioned room. I hate doctors' offices, and I hate Janet's white dress and white shoes. I can't imagine why Daddy fell for her the first time they met. Couldn't he smell the odor of a doctor's office on her? She must have been wearing her white uniform that day four months ago when she went to his car lot looking for a used car. Her old car had just been stolen. "I'd like to find that thief now and thank him!"—I've heard her say that several times. *I'd* like to find him and murder him.

I watch Janet hold up a folder and call some lady's name. The lady puts down her magazine and follows Janet into the back. I don't dare begin to imagine what kind of things go on in a place like this. I hate it. Sick women make me sick. I almost take off, but that would seem too mean, I guess, even for me.

A moment later Janet comes back out and puts some folders in a filing cabinet, then tells this other woman who works at the desk that she's going to have a bite to eat. "Come with me, honey," she says, beckoning to me. "We're going to eat back here. I brought our lunch." I get up and walk over to her. "Vivian, this is my friend Bailey," she says. "Bailey, this is my friend Vivian."

"Hi, Bailey," Vivian says, smiling. "I've heard a lot about you."

Brother, can't you just imagine all the lovely things Janet's told her about me?

I follow Janet back to a little room that has a desk and a bunch of filing cabinets in it.

"Here—we can sit here and eat and visit," she says. She closes the door behind us. "This is the room where I do the insurance forms." She announces this like it's some big deal.

I stand silently off to the side while she goes into a paper bag and pulls out some sandwiches wrapped in Saran Wrap, two little cartons of orange juice—and two Snickers bars. I'll admit the sight of them cheers me up a little.

"Oh, let me get you a chair. I'll be right back." I wish she would just leave me alone. I'm sure she really wishes I didn't exist. Her life with Daddy would be smooth sailing if I didn't exist.

"Here we are," she says, rolling a chair into the room. She closes the door again. "Now. Why don't you sit here and I'll sit here beside you. And we'll eat." She sounds like she's talking to an imbecile.

I sit at the desk and start to unwrap one of the sandwiches. I'm shivering with the cold. It's the air conditioning, I guess.

"You're trembling," Janet says.

"I'm okay." But my hands are shaking so I can hardly get the stupid Saran Wrap off my sandwich.

"Wait a minute—I'll get you my sweater," she says. She leaves, and returns with a white sweater. I'd rather not wear it, but I'm so cold I don't protest when she puts it around my shoulders. She tucks it in close to me, then pats my hair—for one horrible second I'm afraid she might kiss me, but she doesn't, thank God.

She sits back down and we both start eating our sandwiches, but before Janet can say much, we get interrupted a couple of times by Vivian. The first time she tells Janet that the phone's for her, and the second time she asks Janet if she can please come find a certain chart. "I'm sorry," Janet says to me as she gets up to go look for the chart. "Our time together is going to be up before we know it." That's okay with me—I'd be glad to see this half hour pass as quickly as possible.

When Janet gets back, she sits down and says, "Goodness, if it's not one thing, it's another." She takes a couple of bites of her sandwich, then says, "Well. I want to talk with you first about the party on Sunday. My sister, Lynette, is having a little party for me and Dean the night before the ceremony, and I was wondering if you'd like to help us prepare for it."

I barely shrug in reply to her invitation. What does she mean, "help prepare"? Scrub the floors for her? Ha.

Janet puts down her sandwich, then brushes away some crumbs from the desk as if she's thinking about what to say next. I can hear it starting to rain outside. She looks at me. "Honey—I love your daddy very much."

Oh, please.

"I know you love him too. And I know that you've had a hard time of it. I admire you very much. Did you know that? I think you're a very brave person. You and Claude had to raise yourselves. Not many children do that—at least they don't do it and turn out as good as you two did."

I just stare at her, wondering if it would be rude to abandon my sandwich and start right in on my Snickers.

"Bailey, I've had sort of a hard time too." She laughs a little. "Did Dean ever tell you about my first marriage?"

No, thank God, but I just shake my head and reach for my Snickers. I need it.

"Well, my husband was unbalanced," she says.

I try to unwrap my candy bar as quietly as I can. Rain is beating hard against the windows.

"By unbalanced, I mean he was abusive," she says. She pauses again.

For the first time I start thinking this might be pretty interesting. "What did he do?" I ask.

"He was violent at times," she said. "It was very tough."

I nod, wishing she'd give me more details.

"After we were divorced," she says, "I went through a period where I was very bitter. I never wanted to be with another man. But then I started trying to change my outlook on life by thinking positive thoughts—I mean, I would go around all the time thinking, 'I release the past with love. I am now able to have a good relationship.' "

What in the world is she talking about? I wonder.

"I know it sounds odd, but I had to work very hard at overcoming all my negative feelings. Finally, I'm glad to say, things started to improve, and now everything has changed for the better. For one thing, I'm about to marry your daddy."

She smiles at me as if I'm supposed to say "Praise the Lord" or something, but I don't show any reaction.

"I guess what I'm trying to say is that you and I have a lot in common."

"What?"

"Well, we both care for Dean, and we both have some bitter memories in our past."

"I don't have bitter memories."

She stares at me, and I stare back at her, daring her to tell me what she's really trying to say—that my mother was some kind of terrible person like her husband. "I don't," I say again.

She just looks at me, then sort of sighs. "Well, maybe not," she says. "But maybe you can use the approach of positive thinking to change some of the things in your present life."

"Like what?" Getting Daddy not to marry her?

"Well, like your relationship with the boys, for instance. If I were you, and they were upsetting me real bad, I'd say a special thought to myself—something like 'I'm now in perfect harmony with Petey and Buster. My relationship with them is joyous and filled with love.' "

I just stare at her.

"I know it sounds crazy, sweetie, but it works. You know, there are right ways to go about solving problems and there are wrong ways. When you try to be peaceful inside yourself, that's the right way. But when you beat on Buster's head with a weenie, that's the wrong way."

I almost laugh. *Beat on Buster's head with a weenie.* I can't believe she just said that.

But then some kind of sadness starts to swallow up my sense of humor, and I look away from her. I don't want us to talk anymore; I feel like getting up and moving around. I can't breathe in this room; I'm sitting so close to Janet, I can smell her perfume; it smells like roses or something.

Janet seems to read my mind, because she stands up. "Whew, it's gotten a little warm in here, hasn't it? Are you through with your sandwich, honey?"

I nod.

She looks at her watch. "Well, I guess I better get back to work. I'm glad you could come see me today." She puts our half-eaten sandwiches back into the paper bag. I watch her as she starts to put the other Snickers bar in there too, but then she holds it out to me. "Would you like my Snickers?"

"Yes, thank you." I take it from her. As I start to unwrap it, she smiles at me and then brushes her cool hand across my cheek. I get a strong whiff of her perfume, or maybe it's hand lotion, some kind of sweet-smelling hand lotion. Before I can react by moving away from her or anything, she turns and heads out into the hall.

It's not raining anymore as I start for home, and I'm so glad to get away from that doctor's office, I can't pedal fast enough. I think Janet must have been sitting too close to me or something. I felt like I could hardly breathe. And that stuff about my bitter memories—I know she wanted me to talk about my mother. Well, what did she expect me to say? That my mother's hair is long and wavy instead of dyed red and sprayed stiff with hair spray? That my mother wears too much foundation on her face because she's trying to cover up a few scars left from pimples she had when she was a teenager? That she's a little heavy around the hips?

I remember once my mother and I looked through a fashion magazine together and we discussed this article that showed the right things to wear and the wrong things; it said you shouldn't wear horizontal stripes if you're heavy in the hips; and we laughed hard because Mom had on a skirt exactly like the one they showed in the picture. "Oh, I've been making a fool out of myself!" she cried, and this made us laugh even harder. I loved it when she made fun of herself. Except when she was drunk—then she could go from laughing to cursing to crying and maybe in the process take a swipe at me— not because I was to blame for anything, but because the sight of me seemed to make her hate herself even more.

I'm really eager to visit with Claude when I get home, but as usual he's sleeping late. "Wake up, Tarzan," I shout, standing outside his room in the hall. "Wake up." I try kicking his door lightly with my toe, but he doesn't answer. I kick it again. I'm kicking it over and over again when he finally shouts, "Quit kicking my door!"

I'm so restless, I go out to the front porch and swing back and forth like a lunatic on our porch swing.

Suddenly the perfect person appears to help me get over my craziness—Marlene McKinney. She's driving slowly by our house, and she comes to a stop when she sees me. "Hi, Bill," she calls out her car window.

"Hi, Marlene!" I jump off the porch and run across the lawn to greet her. "How are you?"

"Fine. What are you up to?" she asks.

"Not much." I notice she's looking up at our house. "Munchkin is home, but he's sleeping," I say.

"He's sleeping?"

"Yeah, I just tried to get him up, but he yelled at me." She nods, then looks back at the house without making any move to start her car up again.

"I like your hair today," I say.

"Thanks."

"What kind of shampoo do you use?"

"Nothing special." She looks at our house again. "You think Claude's going to stay in bed for a while?"

"Well, some days he doesn't get up until two o'clock."

"Why? Is he sick?"

"No, he's not sick—at least not physically. He's storing up for the Army, I guess. They'll make him get up in the dark, most likely."

She nods and looks down at her lap. Suddenly I realize she's in tears.

"How come you're crying?" I ask her.

"I can't believe he's really leaving—"

"Me neither."

"I wish he'd listen to me, but he won't—he won't even listen."

"Listen to what?" I'm still dying to find out what happened between the two of them.

"My side of the story."

What is her side? I'm wondering. What's the story, period?

"You don't know what happened, do you?" she says.

"I know some," I say. That's true—I know they broke up.

"So he *has* told you?"

"A little," I lie.

"What's he told you?"

"You know—his side of the story." I can't believe I'm being so sneaky!

"Well, I didn't care a damn about Rod, Bailey. I love Claude! Did he tell you that I begged him to forgive me? That I wanted us to get married?"

I shake my head, praying she doesn't ask me any more questions.

"The only reason I did it was because the way he was acting, I didn't think he cared one way or another. I admit now that sleeping with Rod was a terrible mistake, but I didn't think Claude would care even if I did that!" She rests her head against her hands.

I close my eyes. Jesus. I've struck gold. Frances Pepper would give all her worldly possessions for the privilege of hearing this.

"And then he goes and acts like I'm the worst thing that ever walked the face of the earth! And after I told him I was sorry and I even wanted to marry him! But now he's signed up for the Army!" She beats the steering wheel. "Oh, I wish he hadn't done that!"

"Me too! I'd love it if he didn't go in the Army. Then I could stay here and live with him instead of moving over to Janet's."

"When are you moving to Janet's?" she asks, wiping her eyes.

"Tuesday. It's the last place I want to live."

"Why?"

"I don't know. Janet thinks she's going to be my new mother or something. I don't want another mother." I'd rather live with Claude and you, I'm thinking, but I don't say it—it's too mushy. "You better talk to Claude *soon* if you want to try to talk him out of going, though," I say. "He's leaving Tuesday."

"I know that. I'm counting every minute." She looks in her rearview mirror and tries to wipe off the mascara that's smeared under her eyes. "Well, I'm not going to try and see him right now—I've ruined my makeup." She laughs a little. "I'll try again later."

"Is there anything I can do to help?"

"No, I guess not. Please don't tell him I told you all this. He'll just accuse me of trying to win you over to my side."

"Okay. But please come back," I tell her. "Don't give up!" I touch her arm; I feel like she needs comforting. "Hey, think about this," I tell her: "If life gives you a lemon, you can make lemonade."

She smiles at me as she starts up her car. "Thanks. I'll remember that."

"There must be some way to keep him from going," I say, walking alongside her car as it starts to move.

She gives me a sad little nod and waves. I step back as she steers the car into the street and takes off.

I stand in the street for the longest time after Marlene leaves. Everything makes sense now: Claude's moodiness and his decision to go in the Army—and Marlene's defensiveness and all her attempts to see him!

I run to the back of the house and get my bike. Then I glide slowly through the wet streets, slicing through clear deep puddles and going over in my mind what Marlene just told me. Imagine her going all the way with another guy! See—Frances is right—amazing things are going on all the time, you just have to find a way to trick them out into the open.

I end up riding my bike over to the cemetery. I park it and walk over to this huge banyan tree that stands near the road, and I start climbing it. The tree has these wide horizontal branches, and this heavy moss grows on them and hangs all the way down to the ground. Now, this might sound weird, but to me it feels sort of like a combination of God and a big lovable dog. Before you go thinking I'm crazy, imagine how many centuries this tree's been here. Imagine how many ghosts it's seen, winging past its swaying moss at night, making their way back to visit their old bodies. Ha.

I climb up and get settled under a cloud of moss and leaves. Okay, now I'm ready to think undisturbed about Claude and Marlene. I definitely think he should give her another chance. She loves him! What more does he want? I'm sure he loves her too, but it's as if he won't take her back just to prove a point. Well, I think the logical thing for him to do is to make up with her and then try and get out of going in the Army—and then get a job here in town and live with me. That's what I'd do if I was him—it seems so simple.

But Claude's not like me. His heart can turn to stone if you do bad things to him—or even if you do them to someone he cares for. Claude says he'll never forgive our mother because of some of the things she did to me, like when she'd lose control of herself and hit me, for instance. It's crazy: He won't forgive her even though I forgive her—and I was the one who got hit! I never even think about those times, but Claude thinks about them a lot, I think.

A grackle suddenly flies out of the tree and down to the ground, and I squeal and grab hold of my heart—it about scared the bejesus out of me. Grackles are huge spooky-looking birds with shiny black feathers. They look like agents of the devil. "Get out of here," I say in a low voice. I wave my fishing cap at him. But he stays on the ground right under the tree, and then two more big ones join him. Well, I'm leaving now.

As I climb down from the tree, I'm perfectly aware I'm acting silly being scared off by these big birds, but my heart is pounding—maybe it's partly from being next to a cemetery. You know, the feelings you get from your imagination can be more powerful than your good sense sometimes.

I ride my bike all over, thinking about Claude and Marlene and my mother and Daddy and Janet, and when I finally get home, it's almost dark. Daddy's packing up some more things in the living room, but I head straight for the kitchen and start making a snack for myself. Claude's in there toasting a piece of bread.

"Hey, birdbrain." I smile as I hit him on the arm.

"Hi," he says, looking a little puzzled at my show of affection. But I feel really close to him now that I know the truth about him and Marlene. I just wish he'd let me comfort him and persuade him to give her another chance.

"Where you been, Bailey?" Daddy calls from the living room.

"Out."

"Out where?"

"Riding my bike." I reach for a can of mushroom soup.

Daddy comes and stands in the doorway. "I understand you spent some time with Janet today," he says.

I grimace as I open the can with the can opener, pretending it's harder to open than it really is.

"How was it?" he says.

"How was what?" I shake the can, and the soup plops out and jiggles in the saucepan.

"Your visit with Janet."

I start over to the sink to get a can of water.

"Be still now, honey, and talk to me," Daddy says.

I freeze in the middle of my movement like in a game of statues. This makes Claude laugh. I almost laugh too, hearing him.

"Now don't be cute," Daddy says. "How was your visit with Janet?"

"Interesting," I say between tight lips, trying not to move a muscle.

"Interesting in what way?"

I squeeze out the word: "Insightful."

Claude laughs again as he butters his toast.

"Would you please act normal?" Daddy says.

But I stay frozen—more to amuse Claude than anything else.

"Relax, Bailey! Don't stand there like that!"

Daddy sounds like he might really get mad now, so I relax and look at him.

"Did Janet tell you about the wedding party at her sister's on Sunday?" he says.

I nod.

"You going to help them decorate for it?"

"I guess."

"Well, what else did you talk about? How was it insightful?" he says.

"Well, she told me that there was a right way to solve my problems with Petey and Buster and a wrong way."

"Yeah?"

"Yeah. And then she told me something *really* insightful. She said that beating Buster on the head with a weenie was the wrong way!" I cover my mouth and convulse with laughter.

Claude cracks up too, and I grab his toast from him. "She said the right way was to beat Buster with a piece of toast!" Claude really laughs as I hit him on his arms with his toast. See what I mean about him and me having weird senses of humor? Daddy just stands there, staring at us and looking lost.

Seven

I wake up before daylight. I had the strangest dream just now about me and Mom and Daddy and Claude: We were all looking for something in our old car—this tan Pontiac we had before Daddy got his car lot. I don't know what we were searching for, but something was missing. I was looking under the rubber floor mat when I woke up.

I get out of bed and walk through our house and turn on the lights. It's all coming undone now. Last night Daddy packed up the rest of the books from the living room, and he took down the curtains and dismantled the wall unit in the corner that once held the stereo. Now there's just some pennies in the corner, and some old pieces of Monopoly money in a ball of dust, and a rhinestone earring that must have been my mother's.

I lie down on the dusty floor and hold the earring up to the light. I remember lots of times when my mother cared about how she looked—when she wore earrings and washed our clothes and stuff. But Claude will tell you that there were more times when she never got out of her housecoat, and times when she'd keep our clothes hanging on the line for days, and the clothes would get drenched by the daily rainstorms and then they'd dry in the hot sun that followed, until finally they were too stiff and dirty to wear, and Daddy would tell Claude to take them down and put them through the wash again.

Those days Claude ended up doing most of the housework, and he tried to look after me as best he could. He was always telling me to go outside and play when Mom was especially bad off. After she left us, and I got a little older, I started looking after him too. I'd make sure he was up in time for school, and I'd make sure he ate something before he left the house—the two of us even invented this dish of melting marshmallows on top of peanut butter and toast. We ate that every morning for about a year. Seriously, it was good. I think we'd be very happy living alone together—or the two of us and Marlene. . . .

"Bailey, wake up. What are you sleeping here for?"

Daddy's standing over me as daylight floods through the living room. I must have fallen asleep looking at Mom's earring. Daddy looks worried; he probably wonders if I'm drunk again. I sit up and rub my eyes. "I guess I got home late from work," I say.

"Oh yeah, where do you work?" he says, helping me up off the dirty floor.

"I'm a barmaid at the Sea Serpent Restaurant."

I think this is pretty funny, but he just frowns. "Well, listen, honey," he says, "can you do me and Janet a big favor?"

"What?" I'm too sleepy to be on my guard.

"Can I drop you by her house to sit with the boys this morning?"

"What? Baby-sit for Petey and Buster?" Is he serious?

"She'll pay you."

"How much? A million dollars?"

"Please. Can you do this for her? It's a real emergency. It wasn't her Saturday to work, but Vivian got sick."

"Why don't you ask Claude?"

"We did, but he has an appointment to go by the recruiting office and fill out some forms. He said he'd come by and relieve you when he's through."

"Oh, God. I don't believe this." I head off to my room to get dressed. "She better not be planning on making this a habit."

"Don't worry, she's not. Hurry up—I'll be waiting for you in the car."

I feel as if I'm going to my execution as Daddy and I head up Janet's walkway. How in the world did I get talked into this? Forget Petey and Buster; I hate baby-sitting in general. It's been my experience that small children never do what I say. They just bore me to tears with dumb jokes, or they try to drag me into all their stupid games.

As soon as we step into Janet's split-level brick

house, the twins descend on Daddy like he's their long-lost love. "Hi, Dean! Hi, Dean!" He stoops to greet them and they climb up onto his knees.

Janet hurries into the room. "Oh, Bailey! Thank you a million times! Vivian got sick and couldn't go to work at the last minute. Hi, sweetie." She manages to kiss Daddy's cheek somewhere between the tangle of the boys' arms. Boy, they're all one happy little family, aren't they? I feel like the hired help that just got off the boat.

I leave the living room and wander back to the kitchen. I have a sick desire to see if Janet's got any new sayings on her refrigerator. Oh, good: "With the faith of a mustard seed, you can move a mountain," and "God, grant me the serenity to accept the things that I cannot change, the courage to change the things I can, and the wisdom to know the difference."

Please. Spare me. I'd like to pencil in "Dry up" and sign it "God."

"Okay!" Janet says, as she bustles into the kitchen and gets her lunch and pocketbook off the counter. I quickly move away from the refrigerator. I don't want her to think I'm trying to get any wisdom from reading her dumb quotes. "Honey, the boys will be fine playing outside. I just like someone here in case of an emergency and to help them get their lunch. There are some sandwiches already made in the fridge and some milk."

I look around the kitchen while she paws through her pocketbook looking for her keys. Her kitchen is spic-and-span as usual and bright with sunlight. I can't get over how she's got all these mushroom knickknacks everywhere—a clock in the shape of a mushroom, mushroom potholders, and a mushroom toothpick holder. Plus some wooden cutouts of mushrooms are hanging on the wall.

"So just make yourself at home," she says. "You can watch TV or whatever. Or you could study your new room and decide how you'd like your furniture arranged in there."

"Janet, we better go," Daddy calls from the living room.

"Coming. 'Bye, honey. Thanks so much. I'll call you later. If you need me, the number's by the phone." She takes off, and a moment later I hear her and Daddy bang out the front door. Petey and Buster must have followed them out, because I can hear them running around the outside of the house.

Inside, the house is very quiet. I didn't expect to come over here and find myself all alone. I go in and look around in the little den that's going to be my room. I can't picture all my junk in here. Janet's house is so orderly: The walls are real clean, and everything has its own place, and there's wall-to-wall shag carpeting every-where. I prefer our messy house. This house smells like the inside of a vinyl book bag. I can hear Janet now: "Hon, straighten up your room," or "Hon, don't you think you should take a bath? Your feet are mighty dirty." Someone will have to tell her to keep out of my way and let me live my own life. I don't want her acting like she thinks she's my mother. No one's ever taken care of me, except for Claude. And I don't even need him now. At least that's what he seems to think.

I watch cartoons on TV for a couple of hours. I can't believe it, but Petey and Buster don't come into the house at all, except to go to the bathroom. You'd think they'd just love watching big ugly guys blow each other up, but they seem to be trying to avoid me entirely. I don't know if they're scared of me or just hate me, or both.

I finally go and stand on the back steps and watch them play. They're maneuvering little *Star Wars* toys around in the dirt and doing these silly voices for Darth Vader and Luke Skywalker as they try to mow down some ants. They don't even glance in my direction.

I go back into the TV room and sit back down. I don't know when I've felt so lonely before. I wish Claude would get here.

After a little while I go outside again and sit on the steps and just sort of watch Petey and Buster. They're arguing with one another about who gets to have Darth. "Quit," I tell them.

They both look over at me with surprised expressions.

"Be nice," I say.

"You're not our mother," Petey mumbles.

"What'd you say?" I ask ominously as I stand up.

He glances at me, looking a little scared.

"What'd you say?" I ask again.

Petey looks away and pretends to be concentrating on his trucks. I sit back down.

"She can't tell us what to do," Buster says to Petey.

"What'd you say, Buster?" I ask, standing up again.

He giggles, then Petey giggles. They ignore me as they keep playing. I wish they'd at least fight with me.

I get up and go back in the house and just stare out the front window for a while, wishing Claude would show up. Then I go upstairs and look in all the bedrooms. Janet's room is mostly done in yellow with orange-and-yellow flowered curtains. Cheerful, to say the least. I peek out her window to make sure the boys are busy playing, and then I begin opening her bureau drawers. I'm hoping I'll find something secret—such as birth control pills or a *Playgirl* magazine or a diary—but I don't find anything.

Back downstairs I sit in the TV room again, actually wishing the boys would come inside and play.

Suddenly the front door opens, and I hear Claude's voice. I leap off the sofa, and in about ten seconds I'm crashing into him like a wild beast, screaming, "Eeeeh!"

"What's wrong?" he says, sounding alarmed.

"Nothing," I say, punching him lightly in the stomach.

"Oww—quit it!" he says.

"What took you so long?" I ask, jumping up and smacking the back of his head.

"Quit. Nothing. Where're the boys?"

"Out back."

He starts for the back and I follow him, boxing his back with my fists. "Quit hitting me," he says.

"What did they make you do?" I ask. "Take a physical?"

"No, I've already done that. I just had to fill out some forms." He opens the back door.

"Hi, Claude!" both of the boys shout.

"Hi, guys."

The boys start to stand up. "Quick, come in and close

the door," I tell Claude, pulling him back into the house so I can have him all to myself. "Make them stay outside—they've been driving me crazy!"

Claude and I sit in the TV room and watch an old movie. I jabber to him about the characters, and at one point I get so worked up, I actually start beating him with a couch pillow when two of the characters, George and Mary, finally kiss—they've been trying to get together their whole lives! "Quit it!" Claude says, grabbing the pillow away from me.

"Oh, George, I love you!" I squeal and I hurl myself off the couch onto the shag rug.

I keep lying there like a dead fish, thinking I'd give my right arm to keep Claude in town.

Actually Claude seems sort of depressed about his visit to the Army recruiters. He's all slouched down in his seat, and several times he's heaved big sighs and rubbed his hand across his face. I can tell his thoughts are a million miles away.

"What's wrong?" I ask from my position on the floor.

He just looks down at me for a moment, as if he's trying to decide whether or not to share his burdens with me. I don't move a muscle as I silently will him to talk to me.

"I guess it's just beginning to hit me what I'm in for," he says.

I get up and crawl swiftly over to the TV and turn it down. "You mean the Army?" I ask, turning back to him, but trying not to sound too nosy.

He nods.

"Well, it'll be an adventure." I just say this so he won't think I'm trying to talk him out of going.

"Yeah," he says sarcastically.

My heart leaps—God, I'd be in heaven if he was really thinking of changing his mind! "Well, it's too late to change your mind, isn't it? You've already signed up."

He doesn't say anything.

"It *is* too late, isn't it?" I ask casually.

"I don't know."

"You don't know for sure?"

He doesn't answer.

I lie back down on my side and prop my head up with my hand and pick at some carpet threads. "I figured you'd have to go to jail if you backed out now. Isn't that true?"

"I don't know."

"You didn't ask them today if it was too late?"

He lets out a puff of air and shakes his head. At that moment Petey and Buster come running into the house, calling out that they want lunch, so Claude gets up and steps over me to go and get it for them.

I hardly breathe as I pluck some more threads out of Janet's carpet. *I* could ask them, I think to myself. There's no reason in the world why I couldn't ask the recruiters if it was too late for Claude to get out of going. My heart starts pounding. "Lord help us, Weelawnie," I say as I roll over onto my back and stare up at the ceiling. That's an old family joke. It's a line from an outdoor drama that Daddy did the lights for one summer. Claude and I used to say it whenever we were confronted with some real challenging thing, such as diving off a high dive. Maybe I'll go to the recruiting office as soon as we get home, I'm thinking—it's only a few blocks from where we live. Maybe I'll change into a nice dress and walk right over there. "Lord help us, Wee-lawnie!"

Eight

When Janet gets home from work, she asks me and Claude if we'd like to stay and visit with her a minute; she offers to make us all some lemonade. But I say no, I have to get back and start packing. The truth is I'm eager to hurry over to the Army recruiters—I'm afraid they might close early since it's Saturday.

As soon as we get home, I charge to my room and change into a plaid skirt and matching blouse. I've outgrown them both, but they're the nicest clothes I have. I'm so nervous about my plan that I'm actually chattering to myself as I get ready, saying, "Oh, brother," and repeating, "Lord help us, Weelawnie." You know, more people talk to themselves than you might believe.

After I'm dressed, I slip out the front door and start for the street.

"Hey, Bailey! Where you going?" Frances Pepper calls out from a chaise lounge in our backyard where she's sunning herself and painting her toenails. Her own backyard is too shady for sunbathing. "How come you're so dressed up?" she shouts.

I hurry to her so she'll stop hollering—I don't want Claude to hear.

"Where you going?" she asks as she lifts the paint-brush from her toenails. She's coloring them bright red.

"Nowhere."

"Could you do me a favor—look and see if I have a rash on my back. It itches. I think I get sun poisoning from the sun in your yard. I never get it when I'm at the beach."

I'd like to tell her not to blame our sun for her itches —she's lucky I allow her to put her chair on our property in the first place.

"You don't have a rash," I tell her as I peer at her back.

"Good. So why are you so dressed up?" she says.

"I have to do something."

"What?"

"It's a secret."

"It is? Oh, please tell me. If you tell me, I'll tell you a bigger secret."

I sit down on the end of the chaise. "What?" I ask.

"Tell me yours first," she says.

I just stare at her and shake my head.

"C'mon, what is it? If you tell me, I'll tell you a great secret."

"No, tell me yours first," I say.

"No. Tell me yours."

"Well, tell me what yours is about."

"I'll tell you the meaning of a new word."

"What is it?"

She screws up her face and whispers, "Nookie."

"Forget it, that's old news," I say wearily, and I get up to go.

"Wait!" she begs. "Wait, wait, wait—"

I stop. I'm thinking now I probably will tell her my secret, but I might as well get a good trade out of it. "What?" I ask, trying to sound completely bored.

"I'll tell you another word."

"What? Hurry."

"Prophylactics."

"Bye-bye," I say cruelly. I wave over my shoulder as I start to walk off. I'm having a ball now.

"Wait!"

I stop and let my shoulders slump and my head fall forward as if I'm really, really bored. "What?" I ask.

She's hobbling across the grass on her heels so she won't smear her toe polish. "Wait—don't go."

"Well, then tell me something I don't know," I say.

"Okay. What about circumcision?"

"What?"

"If I tell you what it means, will you tell me your secret?"

This really is a word I've never heard of. "Okay," I say. "But it better be good."

"Well, when a boy's a baby, they take his thing and cut it and it pops out."

"*What*? What boys?"

"I think all boys."

"That's crazy! What do you mean—it pops out?"

"Just what I said." She sounds a little desperate. I

can tell she doesn't know any more than what she's told me. Some little kid's probably passed this half-baked information along to her, and she's stuck with trying to figure it out too.

But I'd have to be really mean to leave her now. "Okay, I'll tell you," I say in a fed-up voice. "I'm on my way to have an important talk with some people."

"What people?"

"The Army."

"The Army?" she asks loudly.

"Shhh—I want to see if it's too late for Claude to get out of going. He doesn't know, so don't tell him."

"That's *it*? That's your secret?"

"It's important!" I say, but she doesn't look very impressed.

"You'd like him to stay in town, wouldn't you?" I ask. "You told me once you were in love with him. Well, if he goes in the Army, you'll never see him again, ever."

"Oh." She looks like she's never thought of that before.

"Now you see why it's important?"

She nods. "Can I come?" she says.

"I guess so. But you better hurry—it's already five o'clock—they're probably closing soon."

"Okay—wait a second!" She takes off and runs to her house—*skips* is more the word; she's forgotten her wet toenails, she's so excited.

I make Frances wait outside while I go alone into the recruiting office. It's in a little glassed-in building off the town square. Two men wearing uniforms are sitting at their desks.

"Hello, little lady," one of them says when he sees me.

He looks friendly enough; he has a red face and a squashed-in nose. "You want to sign up for the Army today?" Both men smile, making me feel less nervous.

"No, sir, I just wanted to ask a few questions."

"What kind of questions?"

"For a Girl Scout project." It's a dumb answer, but it's the first thing that comes to me. "For my Army badge," I add.

"Okay, shoot," the man says, and he leans back and folds his hands behind his head. He's got large perspiration marks on his khaki shirt.

"I understand you can sign up for the Army before you finish high school, and then when you graduate, you have to go in."

The man nods, and the other fellow stops looking at me and starts tending to some papers on his desk, taking some of the pressure off the situation. I go on: "What I need to know is what happens if you change your mind between the time you sign up and the time you get out of school."

He shrugs. "A contract's a contract," he says.

"What does that mean?"

"Well, you can't just say I don't want to go anymore." My heart sinks. "Oh."

"Course the Army might not want you if you really don't want to go," he says.

"It might not?"

He shakes his head.

"What kind of excuses would they accept?"

He shrugs. "A law violation."

"What kind of law violation?"

"Well, we just had a boy about to go in who couldn't because he stole a car."

"Oh. And what else might keep you out?"

"Illness . . ."

"What about if you go crazy?" I ask.

"Yeah." He laughs. "I reckon that'll get you out too. The Army doesn't want you if you're crazy. Bill over there's an exception, hey, Bill?" The other guy looks up from his papers and says, "Huh?"

"I just told her you were an exception to the crazy rule, isn't that right?"

Bill just sort of smiles, then goes back to his papers as if he's a little tired of living with this guy's jokes.

"Any more questions, young lady?" the guy asks me.

"I just wondered what other excuses would get you out of going."

"Hey, what kind of badge is this? A badge on how to get out of the Army?" He laughs.

I try to laugh too, but I can feel my face getting hot. "No sir. I just wondered if you could get out if you wanted to go to college or a technical school, maybe."

"Probably. It's up to your commander ultimately. But the two of you could most likely work it out."

"And just one more thing—what if a father leaves his family and you're needed to take care of your younger brothers and sisters? Can you get out because of that?"

He yawns and nods. "I reckon."

"You think the commander would approve of that reason?"

He closes his eyes and nods, and then he yawns again.

"It doesn't sound as if they're very strict," I say,

faking a yawn to seem casual. "I mean about making
you stay and all. I thought you'd go to prison or something if you backed out."

The guy grins. "That would be too much trouble for
everyone concerned, don't you think?"

"I guess so. So what you're saying is basically that
if you don't want to go, there are lots of ways to get out?"

"Yep. I guess there are."

"Well, thank you," I say, my heart pounding. " 'Bye."

" 'Bye." He nods and then closes his eyes again. The
other guy looks up and smiles and waves good-bye. The
two of them seem unusually relaxed and good-natured
—I wonder if they're told to act that way on purpose so
the Army won't seem so scary.

Frances is waiting for me on the curb when I come out.
"Oh boy—come on!" I whisper excitedly, grabbing her
by the arm and pulling her along toward home.

"What happened?"

"It's possible for Claude to get out of going in the
Army! He just needs to talk to a commander or something. But he has to do it soon!"

"Why?"

"Because he's leaving for training camp in just three
days—he has to get out of going on Monday!"

"Does he want to get out of going?"

"I think so. I think he just might. I can't tell for sure.
I need to tell him what they said."

"You better hurry."

"I know, I know. Lord help us, Weelawnie!"

"What?"

I laugh. "Never mind. It's an old joke between me and Claude."

When we get to my house, Frances starts to follow me up to the porch, but I stop her and tell her that I'll see her later.

"Bailey . . . why don't you ever let me in your house?" she says.

I shrug. "There's no reason to go in."

"I'd like to see your room."

"What for? It's just a boring messy room."

"Then why can't I see it?"

"Because you can't." I start to turn away, feeling a little indignant that she's being so demanding.

"Come on, let me."

"No!" I start climbing my steps, but suddenly she shoots past me and giggles as she tries to open my front door.

"Don't!" I grab her from behind and drag her to the edge of our porch. She screams as I push her off—an exaggerated reaction. It's only about a three-foot drop.

"Frances!" Mrs. Pepper is coming up her walk from the driveway carrying a grocery bag. She's wearing a white skirt and jacket. She looks nice with her tan and jet-black hair. I've often thought Mrs. Pepper was beautiful, but I don't like her. She acts like Frances is some precious treasure or something. You can tell she just loves Frances to death.

"What?" Frances asks pitifully as she stands up and brushes herself off. Oh, brother. She's not hurt, but she's playing this for all it's worth now that her mommy's here to protect her. I hate them both.

"Come on," Mrs. Pepper says. "Help me with dinner."

Frances walks over to her mother, and her mother puts her arm around her and kisses the top of her head, and they walk up to their house together, without even a look in my direction. I'd like to spit on both their graves.

I bang into our house, and as I head down the hall, loud music starts coming from Claude's room. "Claude! Claude!" I yell at the top of my lungs.

"What?" he says, sounding annoyed as he throws open his door.

I just stand in the shadowy hall and look up at him, trying to figure the best way to tell him about what the Army guys said.

"What's wrong?" he says.

He sounds so cross, I decide to wait and tell him later. "Nothing."

"Why were you yelling for me?"

I just grin like a fool and try to seize on something to say. "Your music is too loud."

He stares at me as if I'm crazy. "Is it bothering you?"

I nod.

"Then I'll turn it down." He turns to go.

"Hey, you want to go to the pier?" I ask, thinking the pier might be a good place to talk with him about my visit to the recruiters.

"No—I don't have time. I have to pack," he says as he starts to pull his door shut.

"Oh, please," I say, grabbing the doorknob. I don't want him to disappear back into his room and leave me alone in the empty, shadowy house—I don't want to go into our kitchen by myself and fix something dumb to eat. I don't want him to pack. I feel like I'll die of loneliness if he closes his door. "Come on. You're leaving soon," I tell him.

He sighs and lets go of his door and steps back into his room. I follow him and sit down on his bed.

"You want me to pack that picture with my stuff?" I ask, pointing to his *Autumn Leaves* picture.

He doesn't answer as he turns down his stereo and then sits on the bed next to me. "Bailey, why wouldn't you let Frances in the house just now?"

"What?"

"I heard you arguing with her on the porch."

"Oh. Because I don't like to have friends in our house, that's why," I say.

"That's weird."

"Well, where are *your* friends? You never bring friends home either."

"Marlene used to come over a lot."

"Well, she was the only one."

Our eyes lock. "There's nothing for you to be ashamed of anymore," he says. "Mom's not going to magically appear again and stumble naked around the room or anything."

"Shut up. She wasn't naked," I mumble. I get up and walk over to his *Autumn Leaves* picture and pretend to study it. He's referring to a time years ago when I was in the third grade and I had some friends over for my birthday and Mom got drunk and took off her clothes down to her underwear. "Can I keep this for you?" I ask him, touching the rough oil paint on the picture.

"Yeah. Don't change the subject. Mom's not around to embarrass us anymore," he says.

"I know—but *you* will!" I say loudly. I really want to get off this subject now. What's the point in remembering that time? I go over to him and punch him. "I'm afraid you'll start acting like an ape. Whoo—whoo." I punch him again.

"Quit! That's another thing—how come you're hitting me all the time?" he says. He still sounds so serious; I want him to lighten up.

"I can't help it," I say, trying to box with him. "You need to get tough—I'm trying to toughen you up for the Army."

"Don't! Stop!" he says.

"Then-go-to-the-pier-with-me," I say, emphasizing each word with a swipe at his springy hair. "It-might-be-our-last-time."

"Okay, okay. Later. In a little while. Now quit!" he says, laughing in spite of himself as he pushes me out the door.

Nine

The wind is blowing pretty hard as Claude and I lick our chocolate ice-cream cones. We're leaning against the wooden railing of the pier, staring at a shimmering path of moonlight that stretches out over the water.

"It looks like you could follow that path all the way to another country," I say.

"Yeah."

Some fishermen are down the pier buying bait at the little pier shack. The pelicans don't seem to sit on the roof of the shack at night. "Where do you think pelicans go at night?" I ask Claude.

"The Mud Club in Lauderdale."

I laugh out loud, spilling ice cream on my wrist. I

lick it up, then say, "Has chocolate always been your favorite flavor?"

"Pretty much."

"Hey—Daddy never liked potato salad, did he? And he never used to like Tab, either."

"Well, people change their minds."

Neither of us says anything for a moment. The strong ocean breeze is blowing our hair back, and my unzipped sweatshirt jacket is flapping behind me. I feel as if I could circle pretty close to Claude's feelings right now because of the distraction of the wind—it might just keep him from realizing how close I'm getting. "Claude."

"What?"

"I went to talk to the Army today, and I asked them what would happen if a person changed his mind about going in."

"You what?"

"I didn't use your name or anything. I said I was asking for a Girl Scout project—for my Army badge."

He tosses his half-eaten cone overboard into the water. "Bailey—"

"Wait—let me finish. They said you could get out of going if you wanted to. If you acted fast, there's several ways that—"

"Bailey—"

"*Several* ways you can get out. They said you needed to talk to a commander and—"

"Bailey, stop! Listen to me."

I don't want to listen to him. Just the tone of his voice tells me what he's about to say isn't good.

"I don't want to get out of going in the Army," he says.

"Really?"

He nods.

"You're completely dead set on going?"

"Yeah."

The wind blows a chunk of my hair right into my ice cream. I don't care—I don't want any more anyway. I swear as I throw my cone over the railing to join Claude's in the ocean below. Nothing works with him— not all the caution and circling in the world. He's leaving no matter what.

"I have to go," he says. "So I can study meteorology."

"Can't you study that in some school? Is the Army the only place in the world you can study it?"

"I can't afford to go to school."

"Is that the only reason you're going, then—so you can study the stupid weather?"

He looks out at the water. "No."

"Ha. The main reason is because of Marlene, isn't it?" He turns sharply, but before he can tell me to shut up, I go on, "Oh, God, Claude!" I hit my hand against the wooden railing, like Marlene hit the steering wheel of her car yesterday. "Marlene loves you!"

"Bailey," he says in a warning voice.

But I don't care about hurting him right now. "Claude, she loves you *so* much! Can't you give her another chance?"

"I don't want to talk about this," he says, and he starts walking down the pier. God, I could kick his butt —I could throw him over the railing into the ocean. I hate that unforgiving streak in him.

"Claude!" But he doesn't stop till he gets to the end of the pier where the night fishermen are gathered.

I dig my hands into my pockets as I walk to join him.

Neither of us speaks—we just stand there watching the men talk and laugh as they bait their lines and lower them into the dark water. It's all I can do to keep myself from saying anything more about Marlene to him. I don't want him to suspect that she told me about sleeping with that other guy. But she really loves Claude—I believe her. And can't you just tell he loves her too? They're driving each other nuts! If that's not love, then I don't know what is.

It's almost ten o'clock when we get back home, and believe it or not, Daddy's there. I thought sure he'd be all snuggled in over at Janet's, but he's pulled out all the suitcases from the hall closet, and he's got a bunch of boxes stacked in our now nearly empty living room. "We've got to do some serious packing tonight, kids," he says. "Tomorrow's the only day we've got left."

Claude and I go down to the basement and haul up a set of old blue suitcases. Daddy asks me to take them outside and let them air out, so I reluctantly haul them out to the front porch and open them up. Each one has a green satin lining with side pockets; I check the pockets in the first one and find a pack of Handi-Wipes and some rusty bobby pins. In the next one I find two small silver keys and an emery board and a row of old black-and-white photos, the kind you get made in a booth for a bunch of quarters.

In the first two pictures Claude and I have our heads together, and we're both making silly faces. We look awful—he's got spots on his face and I'm missing a tooth. In the next two pictures Mom and Daddy have their heads together, and in one of them Daddy's got his eyes crossed and Mom's sticking out her tongue. But in the next one they both look blank, as if they got caught trying to think of what face to make next.

"Look what I found," I say as I carry the row of pictures inside to Daddy.

"What?" He's up on a stepladder, trying to take down the white paper globe that covers the ceiling light in the living room.

"Look," I say, reaching up to him.

"I can't right now, Bailey."

I wait as he carefully moves the lantern away from the light. Then he hands it to me and I give him the pictures. I watch him as he looks at them. His blond curly hair's shining like a halo under the naked bulb overhead. "Lord," he says, "don't we look ugly?"

Claude walks over and glances at the pictures. "Yuk," he says, then walks away.

I grab the pictures back from Daddy. "We don't look ugly! You guys are mean."

I go back out to the porch and sit on the steps. It's our next-to-last night in this house where the four of us once lived together, for better or worse. And if I wasn't so sure of what to expect, I'd call my mother right now and talk to her about it. I'd tell her about these pictures and tell her that I found one of her rhinestone earrings. I'd tell her about my visit to the Army recruiter, and about my desire to keep Claude from leaving, and I'd ask her to send me a new photograph of herself, a large color photo taken by a real photographer. Well, it wouldn't hurt to just try, I think, and I get up and go inside.

"Take one of those bigger boxes and start packing up

the things in your room, honey," Daddy tells me. He's on all fours, reaching under a hall table trying to unplug a lamp.

"In a minute. I have to do something first."

I get the phone from the hall and carry it into my room and close my door and dial my mother's number. My mouth's a little dry—I wish I'd drunk some water first. I start to hang up so I can get some water before I talk to her, but then she answers on just the second ring. "Hello?"

"Hi, Mom."

"Hi."

"It's Bailey."

"Hi, Bailey."

"How are you, Mom?"

"Fine."

"What are you doing right now?"

"I'm going to wash some vegetables. I got them at the farmer's market this afternoon."

"Oh, that sounds good. Did Charlie come back?"

"No."

Neither of us says anything for a moment. "Guess what. We're packing. You know we're moving on Tuesday?"

"I didn't know it was that soon."

"Too soon." I laugh, but she doesn't make a response. "I don't want to move. . . . I'd rather live with just Claude. . . . I don't like Janet, you know. . . ." She still doesn't say anything, so I go on, "She's the woman Daddy's marrying Monday, remember? I told you about her."

She doesn't answer, and I start to panic a little—just

a moment ago she sounded so good talking about the vegetables. "Mom?"

"What?"

"Are you still there?"

"Yes."

"Oh, I couldn't hear you breathing. Guess what—I found some old pictures in a suitcase. You were sticking out your tongue." I laugh. "And I found an earring. Have you missed a little rhinestone earring? I found it in the corner of the living room where the stereo shelves used to be. You know which one I mean?"

She doesn't answer.

"Mom!"

"What?"

"Are you there?" I nearly shout—I can't help it. Why doesn't she talk to me?

"I'm here," she says.

But I don't feel like going on now. "Well, 'bye. I better go—I'll talk to you later." I hang up and beat my fists against my bed. Just once—just once I'd like for us to have a decent conversation! Why can't she talk to me or answer me or anything? Anything! I feel like bouncing the phone off the wall.

"Bailey?" Daddy says, knocking on my door.

"What?" I shout. I'm mad at everybody now.

"You going to come get a box and start packing up your things?"

"Yes! Yes! Don't worry!" I storm out into the hall, grab a box, return to my room, and slam my door. "I'm packing! I'm packing! Satisfied?" I say to the air. "Get out of here!" I kick a bunch of junk out of my way and throw open the door to my closet.

I pick up a pair of ratty sneakers and hurl them across my room. No point in packing them. I hardly ever wear shoes anymore. Next I grab a bunch of crummy old belts lying on the floor and toss them out of my closet— it's like hurling snakes out of a pit—and I throw out some coat hangers and old Barbie doll clothes and an empty Snoopy stationery box. Then I pull out an old shoe box that holds some of my treasures.

I haven't looked in this box for a long time. I kneel down on the floor and lift the lid. There are some religious things I've saved—when I was small, Mom went through a born-again phase, and she gave me some pamphlets on the subject and a tiny New Testament and a glass ball that holds Jesus on the cross—it snows when you turn it upside down. I guess someone was trying to prove that Jesus can die for your sins in any kind of weather. Claude would like this, on account of the snow-storm.

I'm so aggravated with him—why can't he and Mar-lene patch things up? If only he'd listen to her side of the story. If he'd just see her and talk to her. I wonder if they were doing it, like Frances thinks. Obviously, Marlene's no nun. If she went all the way with that guy Rod, then I'm sure she was going all the way with Claude too. Now wouldn't you think that would just make him really want to try and work things out with her? You can't get much closer to a person than going all the way, I would imagine. So how's it possible to get all that private knowledge about somebody and then just take off and leave? It seems so cruel.

Okay, I'll keep all this religious stuff, more as me-mentos of my mother than anything else. She didn't

stay religious for very long. I ought to add her earring
and those black-and-white photos to this junk, I think.
Put them all together in this shoe box and label it with
her name: Betty Evans.

Another thing I could put in her box is a little book for
alcoholics she left behind. I get up and get the book off
my bookshelf. Mom studied it during a period when she
was trying not to drink. It makes me sad whenever I
open it and read some of the things she underlined:
"Most of us are searching for some kind of Utopia. The
truth we have to accept is that it can't be found in the
bottle." I looked up Utopia in my junior dictionary after
I first read that, and it said, "An imaginary land where
the government, the people, etc., are perfect." Well, I've
always known life can't be perfect. I'd like to remind
Claude that people aren't perfect either, and he shouldn't
be so hard on the ones who mess up.

I put the book in my shoe box; then I stand on my toes
and start pulling things off my closet shelf. An old doll
named Sookie comes tumbling down—bald head first. I
pulled out all of Sookie's vinyl hair years ago when I was
mad at everybody. I felt so guilty afterward, I made
bonnets and scarves for her head and slept with her for
months. Then one day she didn't do anything for me anymore—I mean I looked at her and all I could see was this
piece of plastic with pinprick holes all over its head. I
tried to see her the old way, but I couldn't, not after that
one clear insight. Maybe that's how a mother feels when
she stops loving her child.

I sweep some more things off my shelf. Old torn picture books—I wonder if I should offer them to Petey and
Buster. Forget it—toss them! Those boys don't read

sweet little books about trains and bunnies. They like to mow down ants with their Darth Vader toys. If I give them these books, they'll just make fun of them because they hate me so much. I know they'll never pay me any attention—or if they do, they'll just do mean, sneaky things, like search my drawers when I'm not home— make fun of my underwear, or read my diary if I ever write in it. They'll unearth my mother's little alcoholic book and bald Sookie and Jesus in the snow—

"Bailey?" Daddy's in my room.

"What?" I jump, startled.

He peeks in the closet. "It's real late. Why don't you start getting ready for bed?"

"I thought you wanted me to pack!" I yell.

"I didn't realize it was so late—you can finish in the morning." He starts to take off.

"Daddy—"

"What?" He looks back at me.

"It's sad—moving. I'm having a lot of memories."

"It won't be so sad once you're all settled at Janet's. You'll forget living here."

"I know—that's what I'm afraid of."

"Well, it'll be better. Come on now. Let's get ready for bed. Pronto."

"Pronto?" That's one of the words Janet always uses with Petey and Buster. How dare he use it with me? "Pronto?" I ask loudly.

But he just shakes his head and says, "Wind it up now," and he leaves my room—he must sense I'm feeling pretty wild.

"Okay, I will. Pronto! Pronto!" I shout. I kick my closet door shut and lean against it and sink to the floor.

I'm going to be the only one in our family who'll miss the life we all once shared. After Daddy and I move, and after Claude leaves, our whole history will vanish—our family jokes and special words, like "Whoo—whoo" and "Weelawnie." New words like "pronto" and "weenie" will take their places, and the bright, sunny rooms at Janet's house will bleach out all traces of this old life where there's pieces of us still hiding in old suitcases and corners and closets. After I move in with Janet and Petey and Buster, I'll never be able to find my old life or my old family again anywhere—never again.

Ten

The phone rings the next morning as I'm playing this silly game I invented years ago where I pretend that the fingers on my right hand are a family— the thumb is the grandfather; the index finger, the grandmother; the middle finger, the father; the next finger, the mother; and the baby finger is the baby. I'm lying in bed now, whispering their voices as the five of them scurry in and out of my pillowcase.

"Bailey, it's for you," Claude yells through my door.

I'm surprised. I never get phone calls. "Who is it?" I ask, sitting up.

"Janet."

Oh. "Tell her I'm busy—"

"No, come talk to her—"

"Tell her I'm busy!"

"No!"

"Well, thanks a lot!" I drag myself up and head out into the hall. "You just love handing me over to her, don't you? She better not want me to baby-sit again!"

Claude doesn't pay me any attention as he goes back in his room and closes the door. "Hello," I mumble into the receiver.

"Hi, honey. I'm getting ready to leave for Lynette's house now. She's going to do my hair, and then we'll decorate for the party. Can you be ready in about fifteen minutes?"

Oh, no. I forgot all about helping Janet and her sister decorate for their stupid party. It's the last thing I want to do today. "Oh—I don't think I can anymore," I say. "Daddy wants me to pack."

"Honey, I'm sure Dean will let you come. Why don't you ask him? I'll hold on."

Oh, brother. Of course, I know what he'll say. "Daddy, I can't go with Janet to her sister's, can I?" I yell. "I still have to pack!"

Claude pokes his head out of his room. "Yeah—go," he says.

"Who asked you?"

"Yeah—go!" Daddy yells.

Claude laughs and I reach out with my foot to kick him. "Go to hell," I say.

"What?" Janet asks.

I burst out laughing. "I didn't mean you," I say. "I was talking to Claude."

"Oh." She chuckles a little bit herself. Sometimes she surprises me.

"I guess I can come," I say.

"Great. I'll honk."

Janet's sister, Lynette, lives not too far from us in a neighborhood of brick houses that all look exactly alike. I wonder if the kids who live here ever get lost and go home to the wrong family by mistake. That's what I'm thinking as we get out of Janet's car and head around the back of the house to Lynette's shop. Lynette's a hairdresser and has her own little shop in her basement. Big deal. My mother might have been a hairdresser too, if she hadn't been an alcoholic. She likes to fix her own hair a lot, and she cut mine and Claude's when she was able.

We go right in Lynette's back door, and Janet calls out, "Whoo-ee! We're here!"

"Come on down," Lynette hollers from the basement.

As we walk through her kitchen, I'm amazed at how similiar it is to Janet's: cheerful and bright—there's even some mushroom potholders hanging above the stove. What is it with these women and mushrooms?

"Hi, girls, watch your steps," Lynette says as we descend the steep stairs that lead down to the basement. She's standing there wearing a pink smock and shaking a gray bottle. Lynette looks a lot like Janet, except she's chubby and her hair is dyed blond instead of red.

"I'm all ready for you!" she says to Janet. "Sit right down." She slaps the back of a red chair that sits in front of a sink. As Janet sits, Lynette smiles broadly at me and says, "Hi, kiddo! How are you doing?"

"Fine," I answer, and then I walk over and pretend to study some of the hairstyle pictures on the wall. Lynette's the overly friendly type. I remember the first time I met her at Janet's house, she smiled at me constantly and kept trying to strike up a conversation. She drove me nuts.

When I turn back around, she's dousing Janet's hair with this bad-smelling blue solution. It's already hard enough to breathe in this room without that stuff stinking up the place. I'd go upstairs, but I'm afraid I might run into Lynette's family or something. I can hear people walking around up there.

Lynette must sense my restlessness, because she turns to me and says, "Bailey, this won't take long. You can look at some magazines over there if you like."

I sit down in a hair dryer chair and thumb through an old *People* magazine. Janet and Lynette start talking about Janet's dress for the wedding, and I can't believe that I'm stuck here when I could be home with Claude. I have so little time left with him, I feel like I shouldn't be wasting a minute of it. God, I wish I could leave. I heave a big sigh and throw down my magazine.

Janet and Lynette glance in my direction. "Bailey?" Lynette says. "Would you like me to trim your hair when I'm through with Janet?"

My instinctive reaction is to shake my head no.

"You sure?" Lynette says. "I'll do it for free. Why don't you look over there on the wall and see if you can see a style you might like."

Hmm. I get up and cross to the pictures on the wall and stare at them again. I'd never thought you could just choose a picture of a model that you wanted to look like and then look like her. There is one style I sort of like: This girl has these long bangs and her hair slants downward on both sides.

"Do you like any of those?" Lynette asks.

I point silently to the one I like.

"That's real unusual," she says.

"I like it."

"Would you want your hair to look like that?"

"Yes."

Janet's just watching me, but she doesn't give her opinion or try to talk me out of my choice or anything. I'm surprised.

"Okay," Lynette says. "We'll see what we can do."

Lynette moves Janet over to the dryer, then tells me to have a seat. She puts a plastic covering around my neck and moves my head back till she's got it cradled in her arm above the sink. I close my eyes as she squirts some cold liquid on my hair, and then she starts scrubbing my scalp. It feels kind of good, what she's doing—except I'm not sure I like her being so close. She's so close I can feel her breathing on my face.

"There," she says, helping me up again. She dries my hair a little with a towel, and I'm actually sorry the washing's over. But when she starts gently combing my hair, that feels good too. It makes me feel like going to sleep. "You sure you want it to look like that picture?" she says. I nod. "Okay, let's see what we can do." She picks up her scissors.

Janet smiles at us in the mirror as Lynette starts clipping me. I frown and concentrate on my reflection. God, I really look like a shrimp with my wet head and this huge plastic thing covering my body. I close my eyes and just sort of go into a relaxed trance as Lynette pulls at my hair and snips away.

"Okay," she says after a while. "You can look now."

When I open my eyes, I like what I see. I more than
like it: I think I love it.

"What do you think?" Lynette asks.

"It's good."

"Is that how you wanted it?"

I nod.

"It looks great!" Janet calls out from under the dryer.

"Okay, girls. Trade places," Lynette says. "I'll get Janet
combed out and then we'll all go upstairs."

Janet sits down again in the red chair, and this time
as the two of them talk together, I sort of stand close by
so I can study myself in the mirror and also pay attention
to how Lynette's fixing Janet's hair. I sort of have a new
interest in hairstyles now, though I don't see how Janet's
could turn out as good as mine.

I'm a little pleased when it doesn't—but not because
I'm feeling hateful toward her or anything. Actually at
the moment I don't mind her or her sister so much.

When we go upstairs, Lynette assigns me the job of
blowing up balloons while she and Janet get busy making dips and peeling eggs and cutting up vegetables. At
one point Lynette's little son, Tommy, troops through
the house with a couple of his friends, but she sends
them back out to play, thank goodness. Now and then
Lynette's husband, Johnny, comes in and gets a beer and
then goes back to the TV room, where a baseball game is
playing. Lynette's real friendly to Johnny, asking him
what's the score or when he wants lunch. He reminds
me a little of Daddy; maybe it's just because he's wearing
a white T-shirt. He winks at me once when he walks by.

I guess I look like an idiot with my cheeks all puffed

out, blowing up balloons, but I'm kind of getting a kick out of it. Sometimes it's hard getting them going—but then when I pass that initial hard stage, they fill out real smoothly. When each balloon is full and round, I tie off the end with my fingers—Claude taught me how to do that. I mean I don't need to use string like some people do. "Hey, you're doing a remarkable job, kiddo," Lynette says when she looks over at my pile of balloons.

"I'll say," Janet says. "I can't even blow up one."

"I could probably blow up a hundred if I had to," I mumble.

"Goodness." Lynette laughs.

"Where do you think we should hang them?" Janet asks Lynette as she peels the shell off an egg.

"I don't know. What do you think, Bailey—where should we hang them?"

I study the kitchen. "We could put them all together and hang them from the chandelier."

"Oh, that would be pretty," Lynette says. She says it like she really means it and not like she's saying it just to be nice. "I'll get some string."

Lynette leaves the kitchen, and I walk over to the table and examine the food the two of them have been working on. Janet's spooning this yellow mixture now into a hollowed-out boiled egg. "Yuk—what's that?" I ask.

"Deviled eggs."

"Deviled eggs?"

"Have you never tried one? They're delicious."

I make a face.

"C'mon—taste it." She hands me half an egg and I bite into it. Surprise: It *is* delicious.

"You like it?"

"It's pretty good."

"You want to help me finish filling these?"

"Okay."

"Here's a spoon," she says. She hands me a spoon and I sit next to her and start helping her fix the eggs.

"When they're all filled, we'll sprinkle paprika on them," she says. "And then we'll put sprigs of parsley around the plate."

By the time Lynette gets back with a ball of string, we've filled up all the eggs and Janet asks Lynette for some paprika. "Here, you want to sprinkle it?" Janet asks me. I shrug and take the shaker from her.

"Oh, that looks grand," Lynette says.

"Well, it beats canned pork 'n' beans," I say. "That's what Daddy would serve."

The two women laugh loudly—which is more than that joke deserves, I think. But I laugh a little too. I think I'm having a pretty good time.

Just then a car honks outside. "Speak of the devil," Janet says, rising and going to the window. "I bet that's Dean right now. He and Claude were going to drop off a keg of beer."

Oh great! I can't wait for Claude and Daddy to see my hairstyle.

"You want to start stringing the balloons together, honey?" Lynette asks me.

"Okay."

I climb up on a chair, and I'm tying the balloons to the light as Daddy and Claude enter the back door carrying the keg of beer. Lynette directs them to put it in the corner. Then she and Claude exchange hellos, and Daddy kisses Janet. "Your hair looks real pretty," he says to her. I'm standing up on the chair, waiting for him to look at me. "What'd you do? Get it permed?" he asks her.

"Daddy—" I say.

"Yeah, a little miniperm," she says.

"Daddy!"

"Hey there," he says, looking at me, and then he turns back to Janet and starts to say something.

"*Dad*—"

"What?"

"Look."

"Doesn't Bailey's hair look good?" Janet asks him.

She doesn't have to say that—let him see for himself. "Yeah, real nice," he says, but I don't feel like he really even sees that anything's different. Claude's just standing by the door, grinning up at me.

"Daddy—look. I got it cut," I say. But now he's asking Lynette where Johnny is. "Daddy, look!"

"Bailey, don't interrupt," he says.

"Well, *look!*" I scream.

"*Hush, Bailey!*" Janet says sharply. Then she softens her voice and speaks in this fakey-nice way. "Don't yell."

Too late. She already showed me a look of pure hate. I just want to get out of here now.

Lynette tries to cover everything up by calling to Johnny, "Honey, come and say hi to your future brother-in-law!"

I slip down from my chair as Johnny enters the room. While he carries on joking about this being Daddy's last day as a free man, I start for the back door.

But Claude blocks my exit. Without making a sound, so no one will notice us, we struggle by the door. Claude tries to hold on to my arms to keep me from going out,

and I try to move his hands so I can get to the doorknob
—I just want to be out of here. "Relax," Claude says into
my hair. "Relax. I'll take you home."

I stop fighting him and just stare out the window of
the back door. "Dad—we're going home," Claude says.
"You staying?"

"Are you leaving now, Bailey?" Lynette says.

I nod my head.

Janet's staring at me with this sad expression like
I'm hurting their feelings or something, but I don't care
if I am; she hurt me first by yelling at me.

"You guys go on," Daddy says. "Janet'll drop me off."

He's got no idea that anything has just happened. I
don't say good-bye to him or anybody else as I lead the
way ahead of Claude out the door.

Eleven

So why did you get so pissed off?" Claude asks when we pull up in front of our house. It's the first thing either of us has said since we left Lynette's. "Was it because Daddy didn't go on and on about your hair?"

"I don't care if he goes on about it or not," I mumble, looking out my window.

"Then was it because Janet told you to hush?"

I don't answer him.

"She just lost it for a second. Why don't you give her a break?"

"What she revealed in that one second is just the tip of the iceberg."

Claude snorts and shakes his head. "You know, you're too stubborn for your own good sometimes. You won't be satisfied until you've proven she's bad, will you?"

I just stare at him.

"You've invented this whole notion that Janet is a fake, that she's a witch underneath," he says, "and if you keep pushing it, you're going to find a witch—whether there's really one there or not. You're going to force one to appear."

It's sort of interesting what he's saying—I even wonder if he might be a little bit right, but I'm not going to tell him that.

"And you ought to give Dad a break too," he says after a moment.

"Daddy thinks I'm crazy."

Claude laughs and shakes his head. "He just doesn't know what to make of you."

"He's so dumb sometimes."

"Yeah, he is."

"It's not funny."

"Oh, I know. *Come on, kids.*" He mimics Daddy's voice. "*We got to do some serious packing.*" He laughs deeply and hoarsely. I just love his laugh. I can't help laughing a little too.

"Okay, hop out now," he says, giving me a little shove. "I'll catch up with you guys later."

"Where're you going?"

"I have to drive over to Sandy Cove to say good-bye to a couple of friends."

"When will you be back?" Doesn't he realize how little time the two of us have left to spend together?

"I'll meet you and Daddy at Lynette's party."

"Not until the party?"

"Yeah."

I fumble with the handle of the car door, not looking at him.

" 'Bye," he says.

" 'Bye." I open the door and step out.

Just as I'm about to take off, he says, "Hey—you—"

"What?" I look back through the window.

"I really like your hair a lot. You look real . . ." He pauses to think.

"Sophisticated?"

"Yeah." He smiles.

I make a face at him and then run toward our house.

Just as I'm about to climb our steps, I catch sight of Frances Pepper standing on her front porch. She's half hiding behind one of the porch columns.

"Hi, what's up?" I call out. I'd sort of like to visit with her—I don't really feel like going into our half-empty house and being alone. "What are you doing?"

Frances doesn't answer. I guess she's still mad at me for throwing her off our porch. "Guess what," I yell. "I got my hair cut."

I head over to her, but she slips on around the porch column so she's completely hidden from view.

Oh, brother. I hate apologizing to her, but maybe it's the easiest way to get her to talk to me. "I'm sorry I pushed you off our porch," I say.

She still doesn't appear. All I can see are her hands clutching the column.

"Frances!" I try to laugh, but she's wearing out my patience. "I said I'm sorry." I move briskly to see her, but she moves just as fast, and all I can see are her stubby hands moving around the porch column. *"Frances!"* I move and she moves. She's making me crazy. I jump up on her porch and press my hands hard over her hands so she can't move an inch.

"Come out from behind there!" I say, and then I take her right hand with both of my hands and try to pry it loose from the column, one finger at a time. She's strong, but I finally manage to free her hand, and then I start pulling on her arm, trying to get her to show herself, but she's giggling and pulling just as hard in the other direction.

"I apologize," I say through clenched teeth. "Don't you understand, you idiot?" Suddenly she pulls loose from me and I fall backward onto the porch floor as she scampers into her house.

"Go on, go!" I shriek as I get up. "I'm moving anyway, so I'll never see you again, and I'm glad!"

About an hour later I hear a car door slam, and then I hear Daddy yelling good-bye to Janet. I'm standing in my room wearing the most ridiculous outfit. I was packing my clothes, but then I got sidetracked into trying on some old things to see if they still fit, and right now I have on a pair of scuffed-up cowboy boots and a little short skirt and a blouse that's so small I can't even button it in the back.

"Bailey?" Daddy calls.

I manage to get one of my boots off before Daddy sticks his head in my room. "What are you doing?" he asks.

"Nothing—just packing my clothes."

"Is that what you're wearing to the party?"

"Oh, no!" Brother! He really is hilarious. "I'm just seeing if any of these things still fit."

"Oh. Where's Claude?"

"He went to say good-bye to some friends. He's going to meet us at Lynette's."

Just then the phone rings and Daddy goes to get it. A moment later he pokes his head back in my room. "It's for you."

"Who is it?"

"Some female."

"Frances?"

"No, I don't think so."

I can't imagine who else in the world would be calling me. "Is it Mom?" I yell as he heads back to the living room.

"Lord, no."

He doesn't have to act as if that's impossible. She has been known to call me before. Wearing my one boot, I hobble out to the phone and pick up the receiver. "Hello?"

"Bill?"

"Hi!" Marlene!

"How are you doing?" she asks.

"Fine," I say, wondering what she's calling for. "How are you?"

She sighs. "Oh, Bailey, I really want to talk to Claude before he goes."

"I know. I wish you could. I wish you could tell him your side of the story."

"Me too, but I don't know how to get him to see me."

"He's not here now," I say. "And he won't be back for a while—he's going straight to the party."

"What party?"

"A party for Daddy and Janet. It's at Janet's sister's house. Hey, would you like to come?"

"Oh, Claude wouldn't want me there."

"Who cares? *I* could invite you. You're my friend too."

"Thank you," she says sadly.

Oh, I'm so mad at Claude right now. He talks about *me* not giving *Janet* a break? What about him giving Marlene a break? "Listen, Marlene, maybe if you came, the two of you could get off by yourselves and work things out."

"No, Claude wouldn't talk to me."

"He might. Marlene, I think he's really nuts about you. He speeds in the car after he sees you! Or he slams his door in my face! I think you're the main reason he's leaving town!"

"Oh, great."

"No, I don't mean that in a bad way. I think he's leaving town because he can't stand to live here and not be with you—because he loves you so much!"

"Really?"

"Yes!" At least I think yes.

"I didn't think he cared at all anymore."

"He does care! I think he might stay here if you two got back together."

"He can't stay—he's already signed up for the Army."

"Well, it's not too late to get out of going. I talked to a recruiter, and there's ways Claude could back out if he wanted to."

"Really?"

"Yes! Marlene, why don't you come to the party? Please. I'm inviting you. Hold on—wait a minute. Just hold on." I put my hand over the receiver and call out to Daddy. "Daddy? It's okay if Marlene comes to the party tonight, isn't it?"

"Sure," he calls from the kitchen.

"Good. Can she ride with us?"

"Won't she be coming with Claude?"

God, he is so dumb. He hasn't even noticed she's not been around for four weeks.

"No. I told you—Claude's coming straight from Sandy Cove."

"Oh. Okay. Sure she can ride with us. Tell her to be ready around seven."

"Great!" I go back to Marlene. "It's all set. Daddy wants you to come too. Okay?"

She sounds a little breathless as she says, "Well, I don't know. Okay, I guess."

"Great! Now all you have to do is look beautiful."

"But I don't even know what to wear."

"Well, what about that white dress you wore once to that picnic with Claude? I remember you looking great in that white dress."

"Do you think that's what I should wear?"

"Yes!" I'm so touched—she sounds as if she really appreciates my advice. I used to tell my mother what to wear sometimes too.

"Bailey, I don't know about this. . . ." she says.

"Now don't worry," I tell her. "Remember—with the faith of a mustard seed, you can move a mountain."

"You really think I should come?"

"Yes! Yes! Yes! *Please.*"

"Well, all right."

"Great. We'll pick you up around seven, okay?"

"Okay."

" 'Bye." After we hang up, I clasp my hands above my head and close my eyes. " 'God, grant me the courage to change the things that I can change. . . .' "

Twelve

H er house is the pink one up there with all the yard things," I tell Daddy as we round the corner in the big yellow Cadillac he's borrowed for tonight. "Let me out, and I'll run and get her."

Marlene's parents go in for yard sculptures, such as windmills and flamingos and cement dwarfs, and hanging from their porch beams they've got any number of wind chimes jangling like crazy. It feels as if a rainstorm's on the way as I thump their door knocker.

A moment later Mrs. McKinney opens the door. "Hi," she says in a flat voice. She sure doesn't have Marlene's flair: She's a dried-up-looking woman with a thin, stalky neck sticking out from a flowered shift.

"Is Marlene ready?"

"I doubt it. Go on back. She's in the room at the end of the hall."

I've never been inside Marlene's house before. It smells like wet dogs, I'm thinking as I move through the messy living room where Mr. McKinney's sitting watching all-star wrestling. He doesn't even turn his head to see who I am.

I find Marlene's door closed, so I tap on it gently. "Marlene?"

"Come in."

I open the door, and she's standing there looking like a white flower. Her auburn hair is scooped up in back and held with two combs, and her freckled shoulders are bare except for the thin straps of her white dress. The dress fits tightly around her breasts and waist and then falls down gently over her hips and stops just below her knees. Her eyes are carefully made up with green eye shadow, and she's wearing purplish-pink lipstick.

"What do you think?" she says, looking at me with an expression of fear and hope. She really seems to care what I think—me, a stupid seventh grader who's never even been on a date.

"You look like a white flower."

"Oh, God!" She swings her arms and laughs hoarsely. She's too tomboyish to stay a flower for long, but when she was standing absolutely still she was like a white rose.

"Let me get my purse." She goes to her dresser and looks in her mirror one last time. Her room is very neat; it almost looks like a room at a motel, with hardly any decoration and no piles of junk or clothes scattered around. It's pretty similar-looking, in fact, to Claude's bedroom, and not at all like the messy, dog-smelling space her parents live in.

We step out into the hall and Marlene closes her door firmly as if to keep out her parents' disorder. Then she leads the way through the house, and I follow.

" 'Bye, Dad," she says.

Mr. McKinney still doesn't look up from his wrestling match as he grunts, " 'Bye." It's sad, I think. I'm sure he doesn't realize what his daughter's going through right now—that all her hopes and dreams are pinned on this evening.

Mrs. McKinney's smoking a cigarette and looking out the window as we pass through the kitchen. "It looks like it's going to rain," she says in her flat, dull voice. She doesn't mention Marlene's stunning appearance.

"Oh, it does?" Marlene looks back at me in a panic. "Should I take an umbrella? You think it's going to rain?"

"No, I don't think it'll rain before we get there," I say softly.

"You'll be sorry," Mrs. McKinney says as we head out the door. Whew, I think I'd like to get married and leave this house too, if I was Marlene.

The sight of the yellow Cadillac that Daddy's driving tonight seems to cheer her up as we cross the yard. "Oh, this car's so beautiful!" she says.

"You look beautiful too," Daddy says, as he gets out to open the back door for her.

"Doesn't she?" I exclaim.

"Oh, you two are too much," she says, but she's glowing. She's even starting to sound like her old self again.

When we all get situated, she leans forward and pats Daddy's arm and gushes, "So how the heck have you been doing, Mr. E.?"

"Good. How have you been?"

"I've been real good," she says, though I know this isn't so.

"I haven't seen you in a while," Daddy says.

Oh, brother. "That's because you're never home, Daddy!" I say quickly.

"Oh, I'm there pretty much," he says.

"No, not that much anymore." I laugh and look back at Marlene: She's smiling nervously and the corners of her mouth are twitching. I wish I was sure she was going to have a good time tonight and that everything was going to work out all right.

"Well . . . what all have you been doing this summer, Marlene?" Daddy asks. "Working anywhere?"

"Yes sir. I'm working at the Super-Drug near Kmart."

"Oh, yeah? What kind of work?"

"I'm a cashier."

"She works there every week night. That's another reason you haven't seen her much," I tell Daddy.

"So, you still going to come visit us after Claude leaves?" Daddy asks.

"Sure, she will!" I answer before Marlene can speak, and then I look back at her. She's biting her lip as she stares out her window. I poke Daddy in the ribs, and when he looks over at me, I give him a scowl and a swift shake of my head.

He looks a little puzzled, but I think he gets the message, because he turns up the radio and lets the music take over. A soft slow song comes through the

Cadillac's stereo speakers—it sounds fabulous. I look back at Marlene: Her white-rose beauty and the music and the smooth gliding of this luxurious car give me a hopeful feeling that things might turn out all right—I just wish she didn't look so worried.

When we pull up in front of Lynette's house, my spirits take a dive—there's Petey and Buster out front with their cousin Tommy and some other boy, and they're all poking at something in the dirt and laughing.

Daddy parks the Cadillac by the curb, and the three of us get out.

"Hey, Dean!" Buster shouts.

"Dean, Dean! Come look at this monster bug!" Petey yells.

Petey and Buster run up and grab hold of Daddy's arms and walk him over to see the bug. I'd like to see it too, but if I went over there, you can be sure they'd try to torture me with it—put it down my blouse or something.

Meanwhile Marlene looks like she's already being tortured. Her wide eyes are staring at the group, but I can tell her mind's elsewhere. A car drives by and she jumps. "Don't worry—it's not him," I say.

She just nods.

I look back over at Daddy and the twins. Petey's squealing and dancing on his toes as Tommy picks up the bug with the stick. When he tries to hold it up to Petey's face, Petey screams and runs behind Daddy. Daddy just laughs and takes hold of Petey's hand and starts him toward the house. Buster scampers up alongside Daddy too, grabbing for his other hand. The boys totally ignore me as they lead Daddy into the house. Marlene and I follow them like a couple of outcasts.

Lynette comes out into the hall to greet us. "Hi, everybody." She looks at Marlene and smiles.

"This is a friend of ours—Marlene," I say. "Daddy and I invited her to the party."

"Oh, of course. Good. Hi, Marlene. I'm Lynette Hinshaw." Lynette and Marlene exchange hellos, and then Lynette makes Petey and Buster go back outside and play with the other boys. I like her attitude toward small children.

Daddy, Marlene, and I follow Lynette into the kitchen, and a bunch of people say hello to Daddy. I don't even know who they are, except for Johnny and Janet and the minister from Janet's church who's going to do the ceremony tomorrow. Johnny gets up from the stool where he's sitting and greets us, and then he gets introduced to Marlene. Meanwhile I notice that Janet looks sort of surprised and puzzled. "Hi, Marlene. It's nice to see you," she says.

"Hi, Janet," Marlene says shyly.

"Let's go out to the patio," I suggest to Marlene.

I notice Janet's eyes follow us as Marlene and I head out to the patio. I don't know what she knows about Claude and Marlene's situation, but from the look on her face, I feel like she knows something.

When we get outside, I close the sliding door to shut out the party noise and give us some privacy. "You look scared," I say.

Marlene nods and tries to smile.

"It didn't rain. See—the sun's back out." In fact, the

sky's beautiful: It's deep red and has streaks of lavender running through it. It makes everything outside look pink and glowing.

"You look great!" I tell Marlene. I want her to be full of her old personality—call me "Bill," laugh happily, and speak to everyone as if she's known them her whole life. I don't know what else to say to her to make her feel better.

Suddenly the sliding door opens, and Janet steps out and joins us. "How have you been, Marlene?" she asks.

"Okay." Marlene tries to smile.

"Did Claude know you were coming?"

I move toward Marlene as if to protect her. What's Janet trying to do—make her more nervous than she already is?

"No," Marlene says.

"Well then, he'll be surprised, won't he?" Janet says.

"Do you think he'll be mad?" Marlene asks Janet in a hushed voice.

Janet doesn't answer right away. I could kill her. "No," I break in. "He won't be mad."

Janet just looks at me, and then she looks at Marlene as if she's trying to choose her words carefully. "I think he might be a little confused."

Oh, God.

"Do you think I should leave before he comes?" Marlene asks Janet.

Too late. The sound of Claude's laughter comes from inside. The three of us look up, and there he is in the kitchen joking with Daddy and the minister. We can see him plain as day through the glass door. Marlene's face twitches like a scared rabbit's. I can't believe the dread and terror that's in the air now—this sure isn't what I had in mind when I invited her.

Claude glances in our direction, and when he sees us, he stops in the middle of his laugh. Then he steps forward and slides the door open and stares at Marlene. I've never seen such a look on Claude's face before. He turns to Janet. "Who invited her?" he asks. He looks as if he can't understand why anyone in the world would play such a mean trick on him.

Marlene lets out a little cry and pushes past Claude into the house. Janet follows after her.

Claude steps out onto the patio. "Who invited her?" he asks me.

"I did."

"You?"

I nod.

"Why?"

"I wanted you to hear her side of the story."

"I already know her side of the story," Claude says. He looks as if he's about to cry; he's never looked this bad before—not even all the times that Mom upset him.

"I know it too. She told me all about Rod, but I still think you should forgive her."

"Did she tell you about all the others?"

What? "What others?"

"All the other guys she went out with while we were going together?"

"*All* the guys?"

He nods.

"How many were there?"

He doesn't answer. He just walks past me to the edge of the patio and looks out at the brilliant sunset. I go and stand beside him. "Are you saying she cheated on you with some guys besides Rod?"

He still doesn't answer, but I can see he's got tears on his face.

I put my hand on his back. "Don't cry—"

"Get out of here!" he growls as he pulls away from me. He wipes his face on his shirt sleeve.

"Claude." I move around to face him, but he turns his back to me again.

"Just leave me alone, Bailey! Dammit! Bug off!"

"Claude, I didn't know—"

"Just bug off!" he says. "I'm glad I'm getting away from you—you never leave me alone." He wipes his eyes again with his sleeve. "You go and stick your nose in my business—you've got to have things your own way—"

"Claude!" I try to grab his arm.

"Let go!" He wheels around and yells in my face. "You're just like Mom! You like to hurt other people when you're not happy—"

"Claude, I didn't know she went out with—"

"You didn't know—you didn't care—it doesn't matter —you don't think about anyone but yourself!"

I'd like to touch him again, but I know he won't let me. "Go on—get out of here!" he says, and turns away from me again.

I just stand there, not sure what to do. I can't act like an ape now; and I can't push him or box him or poke him. He's never talked to me like this before—but I've never hurt him like this before. And I'm sort of astonished at how I could have done it. For years I've moved so cautiously around his feelings, but this time

I wasn't even thinking about them. I just brought Marlene here, without a question or a doubt. And I made him break in two. He hasn't had much practice crying—you can tell from the way he's doing it. I slip off while he's facing the sunset and wiping his tears with his shirt sleeve.

It's almost dark as I get the key from under the doormat and unlock the front door. I grope my way across the living room and find the light switch and click it on. There's nothing left in this room but dust balls.

I go down the hall to Daddy's room and switch on his light. He's taken down his blinds and stripped his bed, and his suitcases are standing by the door ready to go in the U-Haul-It day after tomorrow.

I slam Daddy's door shut, then go down to Claude's room and switch on his light. His stuff's all packed too: Boxes are stacked neatly by the door along with a canvas duffel bag and his *Autumn Leaves* picture. He probably won't let me have it now, and I don't blame him.

I leave his room and go into the kitchen and turn on the light in there; then I go into the bathroom and turn on the light in there; and then I go in my room and turn on my light. It seems like I'm the only one still living here. Except for a couple of big boxes, my crappy room looks about the same as always—my bed's unmade and my dresser's covered with junk. I've still got posters papering my walls and a bunch of fishing caps hanging on nails.

I throw myself down on my bed and cover my face

with one of my comic books. I hate myself for hurting Claude and Marlene—for ruining everything. I wish I could die.

As I lie there, I make a decision—a decision that feels as if it was made a long time ago, but it's just been hiding, waiting for the right time to break free from the back of my mind.

Thirteen

Dear Daddy,

I'm going to go and stay with Mom for a while. She's all alone now, and I thought it would be a good time to be with her. Don't worry about me. I'm taking the bus and I have enough money. Tell Claude I'm sorry.

Love,
Bailey

I take my pack out to the front porch and tape my note to the screen door, then sit down on the steps to wait for my taxi. Frances Pepper is over in her yard trying to twirl her baton in the twilight. As I watch her drop it and pick it up, it occurs to me that this is probably the last time I'll ever lay eyes on that little fool. "Give up!" I yell.

Frances looks in my direction.

"You'll never learn. Just give up!"

She rests her baton on her shoulders and crooks her elbows over it as she saunters up to my house. "I can do a figure eight," she says.

"Sure you can."

"I can. I did it last night."

"Show me."

She holds out the baton and then suddenly whips it around in front of her through the air—and then she's still again. She didn't drop it or anything. I'm shocked.

"Not bad."

She shrugs.

"You want to come in and see my room?" I say after a moment.

"I don't care."

"Well, it's your last chance. I'm leaving in a few minutes."

"Are you moving to your stepmother's tonight?"

"No, I'm waiting for a taxi to take me to the bus station. I'm going to Miami."

"What for?"

"I've decided to live with my real mother."

"I thought you said your real mother was a wreck."

"She's okay," I say.

"You said she drank."

"Yeah, she does, but she's not that bad."

Frances doesn't say anything.

"You want to come inside?"

"Okay."

She climbs the steps and follows me into the house.

"That's our living room," I say as we pass by the bare room. Frances nods, and I lead her down the hall to Claude's room. "This is Claude's room. It was always real neat." Next I lead her down the hall to the doorway of my room. "And this was my room."

Frances glances in my room and giggles. "It's amazing," she says.

"How come?"

"I never saw such a messy room before." She laughs again, and I laugh too. "How do you sleep?" she asks.

"I just push aside the junk on my bed and sleep."

"How do you get to your bed?"

"I take big careful steps."

She stares for a moment more, then says, "I wish we could have played in here."

"You do?" Suddenly I wish that too. But it's too late now.

"Where'd you get all your fishing caps?" she says, pointing to the dozen or so I've got hanging on nails.

"I just collected them."

"They're neat."

"You want one?"

She nods.

"Pick out the one you want."

She steps on some books as she crosses my floor, and she selects a purple cap that says "Bud and Mary's Clam Bar." She would happen to pick my favorite—but who cares? I'm leaving all of my old life behind.

Just then a car honks outside. "Oh, that must be my taxi," I say.

Frances follows me back out to the porch and stands

by the door as I pick up my pack and head down the steps. " 'Bye," I say. "Good luck with your Dancing Boots career."

" 'Bye, Bailey."

I get in the taxi and tell the driver I want to go to the bus station. As we take off, I look back: Frances is standing on our porch waving, and our whole house is lit up—I left the lights on in every single room. If you were just riding by, you'd probably think a bunch of people were home.

The bus station looks like a home for lost souls. I feel like I've been sitting here forever. A dirty man without teeth is sitting opposite me, and down the row is a woman in tight yellow shorts with pin curls in her hair. She's got two scrawny boys, one on either side of her; they're each carrying a little valise and a Donald Duck comic book. Next to them a wrinkled old woman and an old man are talking to each other. They stop talking and listen every time the intercom blares out what bus is arriving on what track.

My bus is supposed to leave for Miami at eleven o'clock. I decided not to call Mom to tell her I'm coming. I figure when I get to Miami, I'll take a taxi to her place and just surprise her.

As I look at the people across from me, I catch the eye of one of the skinny little boys who seem to belong to the woman in pin curls. He must be around six years old, and his face is streaked with dirt. As we stare at one another, he starts to smile a couple of times, but he stops himself. I like this kid. In fact, I have the urge to walk over and pat his head—like I petted the little head of that pelican on the pier last winter. I can't help but smile thinking this, and my smile makes the kid smile —but suddenly his smile gets cut off as the woman in pin curls yanks him off the bench. I guess their bus was just announced. She yells at him and his brother to hurry up, and then she clutches the kid's arm and pulls him along furiously toward one of the exits. The skinny kid looks so pitiful trying to keep up as he hugs his comic and his little valise to his chest. God, it kills me. I have to fight tears as I watch them all leave.

I glance up at the clock. My bus takes off in about thirty minutes. I wonder what my mother will be doing when I arrive at her apartment. It's silly, but I sort of picture her washing vegetables when I get there. That picture must have gotten stuck in my mind because she mentioned she was doing that when I called yesterday. It seems odd that she was washing vegetables at ten o'clock at night, but at least she was washing them. At least she'd bought them in the first place for that matter. I remember times when she never ate anything but Doritos and Cheez-Its. She'd leave the half-empty bags around for days and then use them to catch her cigarette ashes when she didn't want to move from the couch to get an ashtray. I guess she'll be surprised when I walk in the door. Claude would tell you she won't be glad to see me—he'd tell you that we only depress her— and he'd tell you it's because she's so selfish. But I think it must be because she can't love us the way she'd like to. When my mother treated me bad, she always told me later that she hated herself for hurting me; she told me that she'd try to do better, and I believed her. Sometimes she'd be crying her eyes out when she told me these things. It was hard to stay mad at her—I would just feel sad for both of us, feel sad for everyone, in fact. Sometimes it's hard to know who to blame. Like the mother of that skinny little kid—she was probably trying her best—putting her hair in pin curls to make it look nicer —but on the other hand, she was hurting that kid, yelling at him and yanking him around, and I hate her for that. I hate her guts. I wish I could have saved him.

"Bailey?"

I look up—Janet's standing in front of me. I didn't even see her come in the bus station.

"What?" My eyes are blurry. I hadn't realized I'd started to cry. This bus station is so depressing—that must be what's doing it.

"We've come to take you back home," she says.

I wipe my eyes and see Daddy and Claude standing behind her. From the expression on Claude's face, I can tell he's not so mad at me anymore. Daddy looks real anxious—like he's waiting for me to say or do something wild.

But I can't say or do anything at all. I feel paralyzed. Janet sits down beside me. "Honey?"

"What?" My teeth start chattering.

She reaches out and puts her arm around me. I'm so amazed everybody's come here to save me, I start to shake all over. Janet pulls me to her and holds me tight against her. I don't move away. I just cry. I feel like my whole body's being sawed in half somewhere around my middle. I can't breathe, but Janet doesn't let me go and I don't pull away from her. She strokes my hair, and I let her. I can't seem to do anything but sob into her dress, and I can't seem to stop doing that. "It's okay," she says, kissing the top of my head. "It'll be all right."

She holds me tight for a long time until I'm not sobbing as much, until finally I lift my head and wipe my eyes. Then she helps me up from the bench, and Claude takes my pack, and we all head out of that crummy place together.

Daddy calls Lynette from a pay phone outside the bus station and tells her they've found me and that we're all coming back to the party. Then as Janet guides me out to the car, she explains that she and Claude kept calling our house looking for me until finally Daddy drove them home and they found my note.

When we get into Daddy's yellow Cadillac, Daddy and Claude get in front and Janet gets in the back with me. It's as if she's afraid that if she lets go of me for just a second, I'll slide over the edge or something. She even insists on holding my hand once we're in the car, and I let her; I'm too exhausted to do anything else.

Daddy looks back at us before he starts up the car. "You want to stay here and be our maid of honor tomorrow, don't you?" he says. "Isn't that the reason you got that pretty haircut?"

"Just drive, Dean," Janet says.

Claude chuckles up in the front.

"Okay, I'm driving," Daddy says, and he starts up the car and then turns on the radio. An Anne Murray song is playing.

As we head out of the parking lot, I whisper in Janet's ear, "What happened to Marlene?"

She positions her mouth close to my ear and says, "I had a talk with her—she'll be okay—don't worry."

I sit back as Janet squeezes my hand and Anne Murray is singing "Snowbird," and I stare at the back of Claude's head, at his springy hair lit by car headlights. I guess he's joining the Army, no matter what; and I'm going to live at Janet's house, no matter what; and Marlene probably won't come back into my life; and my mother will always be a distant shadow. That's the way it is. I can't change any of it, so I might as well give up trying.

But someday I'm going to go off and study birds—I'm sure of that—like Claude's going off now to study the weather. In the meantime I think I can force Petey and Buster to be nicer to me; and maybe I'll ask Frances Pepper to come visit me at Janet's—for one thing, I'd like to get my purple cap back from her.

I keep staring at the back of Claude's head, loving it desperately, as Anne Murray sings and the four of us float down the road in the used yellow Cadillac, heading back to the party. What did Daddy mean, I'm going to be their maid of honor? Who's she? What does she have to do?

"How are you doing, hon?" Janet asks me softly.

"Okay."

"Good. We're almost there," she says, patting my hand.

Lord help us, Weelawnie.

ABOUT THE AUTHOR

Mary Pope Osborne is the author of three previous novels for young adults. Her first was *Run, Run, As Fast As You Can,* hailed by *Publishers Weekly* as "sensitive, moving and remarkably honest"; *Love Always, Blue,* her second, was described by *Booklist* as "an engrossing story of family relationships . . . with teenage appeal"; and of her most recent, *Best Wishes, Joe Brady, The Horn Book* said, "Composed with [Osborne's] same clear eye [it] offers a fresh slant and an appealing protagonist."

Ms. Osborne was born in Fort Sill, Oklahoma, and grew up on Army posts, mostly in the South. She currently lives in Greenwich Village, New York City, with her husband, Will.